Chewing Gum and Other Crimes

SYLVIA GUNNERY

Cover by Brian Boyd

Scholastic-TAB Publications Ltd.

Scholastic-TAB Publications Ltd.
123 Newkirk Road, Richmond Hill, Ontario, Canada L4C 3G5

Scholastic Inc.
730 Broadway, New York, NY 10003, USA

Ashton Scholastic Limited
165 Marua Road, Panmure, PO Box 12328, Auckland 6, New
Zealand

Ashton Scholastic Pty Limited
PO Box 579, Gosford, NSW 2250, Australia

Scholastic Publications Ltd.
Holly Walk, Leamington Spa, Warwickshire CV32 4LS,
England

Canadian Cataloguing in Publication Data
Gunnery, Sylvia
 Chewing gum and other crimes

ISBN 0-590-71786-3

I. Title.

PS8563.U553C48/ 1987   jC813'.54   C87-093611-5
PZ7.G68Ch 1987

6 5 4 3 2 1   Printed in Canada   7 8 9/8
                        Manufactured by Webcom Limited

For my sister's children:
Matthew, Katie and Joe.

Contents

1

Miss Rule goes to the Nationals

A few of the students stood and began to walk toward the narrow window of the classroom.

Miss Rule glared and shouted, "Sit down immediately! Do you hear me? Students may not rise from their seats without the permission of the teacher! I said, be seated!" She stomped her foot furiously. The sound echoed throughout the silent classroom.

By now three students were at the window and a girl with a long blonde braid reaching down to the middle of her back opened it as far as it would go. Quietly, with grace and agility, she slipped out of the classroom into the sunshine filtering through the trees. A boy began to follow her.

"Wha — ? Wha — ?" stuttered Miss Rule.

More students rose from their seats and moved purposefully toward the opened window. Others followed and the silent exodus continued.

Suddenly, Miss Rule regained control of her voice and bellowed, shaking her pointer finger, "Stop this nonsense at once! You have not been dismissed! Students will not leave this classroom without the permission of their teacher!" With that, her finger fell off and hit the floor.

Plato walked to the front of the room, bent down and picked up the finger. With a gentle, courteous voice, he said, "We're leaving, Miss Rule. Nothing can make us listen anymore." Behind him, the classroom was almost empty.

Miss Rule looked down at the finger lying in the palm of the boy's hand. She reached for it, but said nothing.

"Come with us, if you want," Plato said, looking over his shoulder toward the window. The sunlight outside beckoned to them.

The desks in the classroom, the pictures of famous-but-dead people, the stack of textbooks teetering high on Miss Rule's desk, the blackboard with its neat yellow handwriting — all these objects suddenly seemed dreary, as if someone had pulled the life-light from them.

"There isn't any reason to stay," Plato added as he turned to leave.

And then Miss Rule was alone. From outside, and growing more distant, she could hear happy voices. A small dog yapped playfully.

She took a half-step toward the window, then stopped. Shaking her head, she put her dismembered finger into the pocket of her long, brown sweater. She walked to the chalkboard and with slow, deliberate movements began to erase the day's lesson.

Turning away, she brushed the chalk dust from her hands and slowly walked down one aisle of the classroom and back up another. As she neared the window, she glanced out. Then she looked back. She seemed to memorize every classroom detail.

Then, awkwardly, Miss Rule climbed through the open window into the sunlight.

Alex gave the cue. The stage lights faded to black and the curtains slowly closed. Enthusiastic clapping broke out, accompanied by a few bravos from admiring parents. The cast quickly reassembled for the curtain call, giggling and hugging in nervous excitement.

The curtains swished back and, one by one, the actors hurried on stage. Finally, with much cheering and clapping, came Miss Rule. Again the curtains closed, but the roar from the audience demanded another curtain call. They got it, and once more.

The backstage corridors swarmed with actors, stage crew, friends and family. With everyone talking at once, Mr. Thomas had to shout over the hubbub. "I'd like the entire cast and crew to meet me in exactly fifteen minutes in the gym," he announced. "The adjudicator will speak to us there." With that, another burst of excitement erupted.

In the girls' dressing room, JoAnn removed the bulky padding she had worn as Miss Rule and fell exhausted into a chair. Patti took out the hairpins holding Miss Rule's gray wig and lifted it from JoAnn's head. Carefully she placed it in a large hat-box. The other girls were busy globbing white cream on their faces and wiping off their stage make-up. No one shut up for a minute.

Alex, the stage manager, knocked on the door and yelled, "Five minutes to judgment time!"

"My heart's thumping right through my skin," said JoAnn to Patti, who was busy organizing the costumes on labeled hangers. "We have to win! We just have to!"

"Relax. I already know we did."

"What? You do? Who — I mean, how could you —"

Patti tapped the side of her head. "I just know."

"Time!" shouted Alex. Patti opened the door and everyone scrambled into the hall.

The adjudicator was already sitting in one corner of the gym. As the boys and girls filed in, a hush fell. People stood as still as statues against the walls or sat quietly on benches. Patti walked over to Alex. Although he thought maybe he should take her hand, or even lean his arm on her shoulder, he simply put his hands in his pockets and smiled at her. JoAnn stood beside them.

As soon as everyone was settled, the adjudicator flipped open a notepad on his knee and introduced himself. "As you know, I am John Stapleton, professor of theater and a former actor. I am honored to judge this drama festival." He smiled. "It is my duty now to comment on your play, 'Rhyme, Reason, and Miss Rule.' Informally, I would like to say that your play delighted me. It was both entertaining and thought-provoking."

Everyone's shoulders slumped in relief, and happy grins broke out all around.

4

"There are two contributing factors to my reaction to your play, a reaction which I know was shared by the majority of people in the audience tonight. First is the playwright, your teacher and director, Mr. Thomas."

Everyone clapped and cheered, but then quickly settled down again in solemn anticipation.

"The other factor is the quality of the production, including the actors and the backstage crew. All quite precise, with, as I shall mention later, only a few areas which require polishing before you take your play to the National Drama Festival in Ottawa three weeks from now."

There was silence. It was as though, for a long moment, the adjudicator's words did not reach the people in front of him. Then simultaneous squeals, laughs, cheers and gasps of surprise ricocheted around the room.

"We won! I knew we'd do it! We won!" Patti screamed to JoAnn, then whirled around to give Alex a hug. Outside in the hall more cheers and noise erupted when it was learned that Joseph Howe Junior High School Drama Club had won the Provincial Drama Festival and was on its way to the Nationals.

*   *   *

Alex waved again as Patti got into the back seat of JoAnn's parents' car. He stuffed his hands into his pockets and started home. He really felt let down now. The news about the National Drama Festival in Ottawa would be about as thrilling to his father as a sale of diapers at the corner drug-store.

When he opened the door to his house, he could hear a voice on the TV shouting something about a fantastic goal.

"That you kid?"

"No, it's a burglar."

"Don't use mouth on me!"

"Just joking," said Alex with a straight face as he entered the living room. "Who's winning?"

"The other guys." His dad rolled a fat cigar around his tongue. "So, where were you?"

"School."

"Something going on at school?"

No, I was just there cleaning out my locker, Alex wanted to say. But, rather than give any "mouth," he replied, "We won the Provincial Drama Festival tonight." No sense even mentioning Ottawa. Tomorrow he'd face the fact that he'd never in a million years be allowed to go.

"Waste of time. Don't know why you're in that playactin'."

"I'm the stage manager. I can't act," said Alex flatly. It was useless to try to explain again.

"Same thing."

But then someone else scored and his father went back to watching the game.

Alex went to the fridge and poured himself a glass of milk. He grabbed a slice of baloney, curled it twice to form a hollow roll, and returned to the living room to watch the rest of the game. But it was hard to concentrate. Mr. Thomas was counting on him to go to Ottawa and he didn't

6

know where to start to convince his father to let him go.

When the Leafs were ahead by one goal, Alex decided to take advantage of his father's congenial mood.

"Winning the Drama Festival means that we're supposed to go to Ottawa in three weeks."

"You already been there when you were one or two."

"This isn't a tour."

"Well, you don't need to go. Teams travel without a manager sometimes."

"I'm not that kind of manager. I'm in charge of lights and sound effects and I set things up on stage and stuff like that."

"Show someone else how. It'll cost too much. And you got your weekend job with me. How am I supposed to handle the backlog of work I have without any help? You can't just tell people they'll have to put off having toilets and tubs."

"You could hire someone else."

"The answer is no. Now, how about another beer for your old man. And you may as well get that look off your face because a no's a no." Handing the beer to his father, Alex tried another tactic. "It won't cost anything. The school pays for the trip and they put us up free in a dorm. I have some saved for spending money, so it wouldn't cost you anything."

His father watched a commercial with a car smashing through a paper barrier to show how much farther it could go on just one drop of gas.

"Uncle Jake is always saying he could use

the money if you need to hire extra help. It'd be the same as paying me."

Now the commercial was for skates, and Wayne Gretzky was grinning over a pair of sharp blades while a kid with too many freckles watched him like he was God.

"I'll only be away four days. I could put in extra time before we go."

One of the Leafs, sweaty hair sticking to his forehead, a towel around his neck, was being interviewed about the last goal.

"Dad?"

"I hear ya. And you heard me. Now drop the subject. You'll forget about this before that fuzz under your nose has a chance to grow out again." And he gave a small laugh to show he wasn't in a bad mood — yet.

*   *   *

Alex waited in the hall outside Mr. Thomas's classroom while a crowd of kids squeezed past three at a time. Someone was still talking to him at the front of the room, so Alex didn't go in. Instead he rehearsed what he'd say, not wanting to sound like a crybaby about not going. He'd just say it straight.

The other student came out.

"Excuse me, Mr. Thomas," Alex said. "Could I talk to you for a minute?"

Mr. Thomas was jamming papers into his briefcase, but stopped. "Sure." He sat down on one of the desks and motioned to Alex to do the same. "What's on your mind?"

"I can't go to the Drama Festival. Dad won't let me."

"Why not?"

"Uh — it's just that — " Alex hesitated, not wanting to make his father sound like a total jerk, because he really wasn't. He'd have to leave the details out. "Dad has his reasons, sir. Anyway, I can train someone else to be stage manager. We've got almost three weeks."

"You're our stage manager, Alex. Would it help if I talk to your father?"

"Thanks anyway, Mr. Thomas, but Dad isn't likely to change his mind. He'd be cheesed off at me if you tried, so I'd rather you didn't. Not that I don't appreciate it. What I wanted to say was I thought Carol Hebb would be good to train. She's the best stagehand we've got."

Mr. Thomas didn't say anything right away. Then he got up from the desk. "Give me some time to think about this. I'll talk to you tomorrow."

"Well, if you don't agree about Carol, then I'd say Billy might be okay except I don't think he'll remember the small props unless somebody bugs him all the time."

"We'll talk tomorrow."

"Sure, sir." As he left the room, Alex felt that something was up, but he couldn't quite figure out what.

When he got home, he saw his father's van parked in front of the shop behind the house. Nothing unusual about that. But next to it was a beat-up blue Pinto. No mistaking that car — it was Mr. Thomas's.

9

Alex did an abrupt about-face and marched quickly back down the street. That was one conversation he didn't want to witness. He hoped Mr. Thomas wouldn't think his father was an idiot.

*   *   *

In the workshop, the conversation was becoming heated. When Mr. Thomas had first arrived, he'd hoped that a smile and some warm words about how skillful Alex was as a stage manager would win Mr. MacInnis over. It didn't work.

"Now I'll tell you something it's clear you don't know much about," Mr. MacInnis said, putting a chrome piece down on his workbench. "Bringing up a fourteen-year-old boy on your own isn't easy."

"I can sympathize with that, but —"

"No buts. You can't know what it's like."

Mr. Thomas realized that listening was the only choice he had.

"Alex was four when his mother died. He barely remembers her. So I'm all he has. The boy depends on me and I got to be careful."

"But surely this school trip would pose no problem, Mr. MacInnis. It's a supervised situation. Besides, Alex has worked on this play all winter. He's counting on being in Ottawa."

"No he's not."

"What do you mean? Of course he is. The whole drama club is looking forward to it."

"Alex has to ask me before he can count on anything. That's the way it's always been."

"But why won't you agree? I can't see any reasonable — "

10

"Reasonable. Now there's a funny word. Means lots of different things a dictionary won't tell you about. Just depends on who's doing the thinking, wouldn't you say?" He had a wry smile on his face as though the young teacher had lots to learn.

Mr. Thomas sighed. "Why talk in circles, Mr. MacInnis? What's the problem with Alex going on this trip? Just say it straight."

"He's too young to be away from home on his own."

"But he'll be with the school group. I'll be responsible for them while they're away and they can share that responsibility."

"They'll share, will they? Fifty-fifty? Forty-sixty? Someone's got to take full responsibility, and what I'm saying is that's my job. I'm his father. So for the last time, he's not going. And that's that."

He turned back to his workbench. "Now the bell might've rung to let you off for the day, but I've still got some work to do."

"I think you're making a mistake."

"You're welcome to your opinion," Mr. MacInnis said without anger. He was already concentrating on the work in front of him.

"This is a terrific opportunity for Alex and you're cutting him off."

"An opportunity for what?" He didn't stop to look up.

"Education, new friendships, a chance to learn self-reliance. He has to start sometime."

Mr. MacInnis leaned closer to inspect the threads of the chrome pipe. Then he scraped

11

something loose with a file. "Plenty of time for all that when he's older."

Mr. Thomas looked away from Alex's father. Then turning back he said, firmly, "You're being unreasonable."

Mr. MacInnis was wrapping white tape around the pipe-fitting. He stopped short. "How old are you?"

"What difference does that make?" Mr. Thomas raised his voice in frustration.

Mr. MacInnis waited for an answer.

"Twenty-six."

"Married?"

"No."

"Then you wait a few years and maybe you'll get married and have a son of your own and you'll have to make decisions for him. Then come back and tell me I'm unreasonable."

"If I narrow my child's life down to his own backyard when he's ready to experience more than I can offer him, like you're doing, I hope someone takes enough interest to tell me I'm unreasonable."

With that Mr. Thomas stormed out of the workshop. After a few moans, his car started and he drove out of the yard.

* * *

When Alex ventured back home, Mr. Thomas's car was gone. Only the van was parked outside.

He went into the shop to find out what had happened, but no one was there. A crate, some smaller boxes and a few chrome pieces were stacked near the counter, which meant that his father was just about to head out on a job.

He walked around to the back door of the house and cautiously opened it. Everything was quiet. But as he entered the kitchen he saw his father sitting at the table, wearing his overalls and drinking a beer.

"Oh it's you, Dad." Somehow his voice didn't sound as nonchalant as he'd hoped it would.

"You sic that teacher on me?"

"What? Who?" It was a good thing he was just the stage manager, not an actor, Alex thought.

"That Thomas fella. You ask him to come here? He said you went to see him today to tell him I wouldn't let you go to Ottawa with that club."

"I just went to tell him I couldn't go. I said I would train someone else to be stage manager. That's all I went there for. I didn't know he'd come here, Dad. Honest."

His father tipped the bottle back and swallowed a mouthful of beer.

"What did he say?"

"What do you think he said? He said you should go and he made me feel like I wasn't much of a father if I didn't let you. Well, I told him when he's old enough to have a fourteen-year-old son of his own then maybe he'll see that letting his kid run off to some kind of drama festival when there's responsibility at home is not the best thing. School trips aren't all he thinks they are. No doubt about that. And I told him so."

"Did he get mad?" Just picturing the scene

made him cringe. His dad had a way with words that an English teacher mightn't like too much.

"Not exactly mad. Frustrated, I'd say." The beer bottle was empty. "Put on your overalls and come on this job with me. Just be an hour."

2

Practice makes perfect

Carol sat beside Alex the next afternoon at rehearsal. They both wore headphones and followed the same script. Even though Carol was picking up the stage managing job easily, Alex couldn't completely put Ottawa out of his mind.

"I want one more run-through of scene six," shouted Mr. Thomas. "Alex, make the changes. We're not breaking. Everyone to their places. JoAnn, where's Miss Rule's cardigan?"

Alex took off the headphones and began scrambling quickly around the stage: write the grammar exercise on the board, coat the brush with chalk for the scene where Gloria blows a cloud in Wade's face, sharpen Miss Rule's pencil to a fine point, put dictionaries in all the desks, open the window a crack, check JoAnn's cardigan pocket for the false finger, cue sound to number forty-seven, cue lights to number sixteen, check the wings for six actors stage left and three stage right.

"House lights," said Alex quietly into the small mike attached to his headphones. The auditorium faded to blackness. "Ready lights cue sixteen. Ready sound cue forty-seven. Cue lights sixteen. Cue sound forty-seven."

Lights glared down on a classroom setting. JoAnn was in place at Miss Rule's desk. The noise of students shouting could be heard in the background. A bell rang with a blast. Startled, Miss Rule snapped the point of her pencil against the page of her daybook.

Exactly twelve minutes and eleven seconds later Alex gave light cue nineteen and the stage lights faded to black.

"Alex, give me full lights, please." Mr. Thomas had been standing during the rehearsal of this scene, and now he was leafing through his copy of the script. "Your words are drifting, JoAnn. Miss Rule isn't quite coming through." He looked around the stage as if trying to find the ghost of Miss Rule somewhere beside the desks or suspended in midair next to the window.

JoAnn stood impatiently with her arms folded. She didn't like to be singled out.

Mr. Thomas continued. "In this last scene, what is it Miss Rule comes to understand that she didn't know before?"

"That she's useless," was her quick reply.

"Useless." Mr. Thomas turned the word over in his mind.

Then an idea occurred to him. "When Miss Rule climbs out through that window, where do you think she goes?"

"What? I don't get the question. She just goes out. Backstage. The play's over."

"But what if the play didn't end there? Where would she go?"

"You tell me. You wrote it."

"Look, JoAnn. If you don't get down off that high horse of yours, we're not going to get any-

16

where. And unless you know Miss Rule inside out, you won't deliver her to the audience. She'll just be a character in a play crawling out the window to go backstage." He closed his script.

"Let's call it a day," he said to the rest of the cast and the crew. "See all of you same time tomorrow."

Then he turned back to JoAnn. "I want you to do some homework. Think about Miss Rule, JoAnn. Seriously. What does she do when she goes out that window? Come to my room at 8:15 tomorrow morning and tell me your answer. I promise if you do this you'll be in the running for best actress at the Nationals. Your Miss Rule will knock them dead."

He smiled, but JoAnn just shrugged her shoulders and headed for the dressing room.

"Alex," he called, "can I see you for a minute?"

"Let's go," said Alex to Carol who was putting props away in a box. "He probably means you too. And don't worry. We did fine."

"Thanks, Carol, but I just need Alex for now," Mr. Thomas said when they reached him.

"I took a liberty, Alex," he continued as she turned away. "Let's see if it did any good." He started down the stage steps into the auditorium and Alex followed, wondering what was up.

Way at the back, almost hidden in the dark shadows, was his father getting up from a seat. In his hands he held remote-controlled headphones.

"I asked your father to come here to have a look at just what it is you do. Thought he'd get a better idea of why we need you."

"Dad — " It gave Alex a weird feeling to

think his father had listened in on the whole rehearsal, including the cues and the near-blunder he'd made when he was explaining something to Carol. He couldn't imagine what his dad would have made of such a strange conversation.

"Quite a lot of whispering back and forth," was all Mr. MacInnis said as he handed the headphones to Mr. Thomas.

"Very important whispering. Your son, here, controls the whole play."

"Carol did a good job too, sir," said Alex. He still couldn't believe that his father was standing there in the school auditorium. But at the same time, his heart was pounding with the sudden hope that this plan just might work.

"Now that you've seen him in action," said Mr. Thomas, looking intently at Alex's father, "will you change your mind and let your son come to Ottawa with the Drama Club?"

"I'll give it some thought. And as soon as you're done here, Alex, you can come back to the shop. I got an hour's work to make up for over at Mrs. Winchcolm's and I'll need a hand."

Alex barely glanced at Mr. Thomas when he muttered, "Thanks for trying, sir."

*   *   *

"Who knows what the old hag did when she stuffed her fat body out through that stupid window?" JoAnn said spitefully as she changed out of her costume.

"Just make something up." Patti knew enough to stay out of JoAnn's way when one of these moods hit.

18

"In one night?"

"I'll help you. Let's see. She goes out the window and . . ."

"Nothing. She does nothing."

"What's she doing just before that?"

"Nothing. The place is empty."

"She erases the board. That's it. And she walks up and down the aisles thinking stuff."

"Like how those padded hips itch sometimes."

"Come on, JoAnn. Thomas said to be serious." Patti had carefully hung all the costumes on hooks.

They hauled on their coats and picked up their books. Everyone else seemed to be gone, but Alex was waiting for Patti outside the dressing room.

"We're just figuring out what Mr. Thomas asked JoAnn to do for homework," Patti said.

"Yeah. I heard him when I was putting props and stuff away."

"It's a stupid idea. What good's it going to do? The play ends. That's it."

"I bet she goes to pat the dog," offered Alex.

"What dog?"

"The one in the sound effects. You know, after the kids are all outside."

"She wouldn't touch a dog with her lily-white hands," grumbled JoAnn.

Patti knew JoAnn was getting hooked, so she added, "Or maybe she'd run after the students and yell something like 'Freedom for —'"

"No," JoAnn interrupted. "She'd feel really stupid after she got outside."

Patti and Alex waited for the rest.

"She'd feel really stupid and would just stand there thinking something like 'What if the principal sees me here and finds out I climbed from the window?' "

"So would she go with the students?" Patti asked.

"No, she'd feel too weird. She never really went anyplace with them before, except the classroom where she had all those rules of hers."

They were now at the small park where the two girls met and parted every day. "I've got to get home. Mom wants me to baby-sit and I'm late already," said Patti.

"Call me later, okay?"

"Sure."

"Good luck with the homework," Alex said without much enthusiasm.

JoAnn walked on alone. Mr. Thomas's words kept going through her mind. If only she *could* win the award for best actress. Only Patti knew her secret about acting: she wanted to go to a theater school some day and be on stage at Stratford, or maybe even Broadway.

The thought that she might stand a chance of being best actress at the Nationals was screaming through her mind. She was determined to know Miss Rule inside out, even what she'd eat for breakfast.

*　　*　　*

"Your father say anything about Ottawa yet?" asked Patti when she and Alex were almost at her house.

"Just no."

"But maybe he'll change his mind now that he saw the play and all the stuff you do."

"Maybe." Alex had a huge twinge of guilt that he hadn't hurried right back to the shop as his father had asked. If there was any chance he'd change his mind, Alex sure wasn't helping much by walking Patti home first.

"You can come in while I baby-sit. Mom's just going for groceries."

"I'd better go home. Dad said he needed me at the shop."

"Ask him about Ottawa."

"Sure." But he couldn't picture bringing up the topic.

"I really want you to go on this trip."

"Yeah." Alex's smile wasn't at all confident.

* * *

Alex lifted his work visor and pushed back his hair to keep it from falling in his face.

"Can you get at it from that side?" Mr. MacInnis asked. They both lay on their backs on either side of the old sink.

Alex turned the visor sideways, adjusting the lightbulb that glared inside its wire cage. "Yeah."

"What's it look like?"

"Pretty corroded."

"Try that wrench on it."

"Can't move around enough to get a good enough grip on the wrench."

"Well then, what do you think?" Mr. MacInnis asked. He waited to give Alex time to figure the situation out.

"We could use the torch to heat the joint first," he replied.

"Now you're thinking."

While his father watched, Alex played the flame of the torch around the rusted joint. "There," he said finally.

"Try it now." He slid his body closer to watch as Alex applied pressure with the wrench. The joint came loose.

"That's it." Alex put the wrench down.

"Couldn't have done it better myself," said his father, as he eased himself out from under the sink.

With only a hint of pride, Alex helped remove the old fittings.

When the work was completed on Mrs. Winchcolm's "powder closet," as she called it, Alex's father still hadn't brought up the subject of the trip to Ottawa.

"When'd you learn all that?" Mr. MacInnis said, out of the blue, as the van neared their street.

"Huh?"

"All that stage managing. Thomas teach you that?"

"Most of it. Then we had this weekend last year when some people from a theater course at the university came with their equipment and showed us how to use it."

"Did you tell me about that?"

"I think I did. A bit of it anyway."

"Mm."

But that was the end of the conversation.

*　　*　　*

Mr. Thomas wasn't in his classroom yet when JoAnn arrived. She waited alone in the hallway, rehearsing the plan she'd worked out and gone over at least six times the night before.

"Good morning, JoAnn," said Mr. Thomas as he approached, flipping through his ring of keys. "Homework done?" He didn't seem to notice that the person standing beside his classroom door was not JoAnn, but Miss Rule. Even without the disguise of costume, it was still Miss Rule.

When she started to speak, he turned abruptly. "Before the students are admitted to the building, Mr. Thomas, I wanted a moment to speak to you about the — ah — incident yesterday in my classroom. I'm sure you know what I am speaking of." Miss Rule's head was high, but her face showed an expression of haughty embarrassment.

"Why — er — yes, Miss Rule," said Mr. Thomas, "I did hear something about it."

"Well, now I'd like to tell you my version. I respect you, Mr. Thomas. We've taught right next door to each other for years and I am sure you've known how I run my classroom."

"Well, yes, after all these years, but — "

"I believe I asked to speak to you. Would you please listen?"

Mr. Thomas supressed the urge to smile. JoAnn was doing a terrific Miss Rule. But it was odd to hear that voice and see that stiff manner coming from JoAnn herself, without the wig and the padded hips and the old cardigan.

"Well, yesterday, my students left my classroom without my permission. They climbed out of the window. It was a rebellion, Mr. Thomas. No other word for it. They wouldn't listen to me. Plato said something before he left about how my

23

classroom rules weren't any good. And then I was all alone."

She paused and looked away. "Well, what could I do? The shouts of my students were loud enough to hear right in the middle of the afternoon." She looked back. "I'm sure you heard them."

"Yes, as a matter of fact I did, but — "

"My heart was just pounding. My rules had been broken. My students had left. I was sure the principal would see them outside. I began to panic, Mr. Thomas. I, Edith Rule, began to panic."

There was no way that Mr. Thomas could hold back a grin this time, but he quickly recovered. "Excuse me, but I'd never heard your first name before, Miss Rule. It's beautiful. May I call you Edith?"

"Yes, you may, Mr. Thomas . . . William." Miss Rule looked down at her hands and dusted imaginary chalk from them.

Then she continued. "Something strange happened. I looked out that window at the sunshine and the trees and the fresh air and I wanted to be out there too. Suddenly I was sick and tired of all the rules. Do this. Do that. Don't do this. Don't do that. I was fed up with making rules and forcing people to stick to them. My hair was gray before I was forty-five, William. And no wonder!"

"So what did you do, Edith?"

She looked over her shoulder to check that no one else could hear, then she leaned closer to Mr. Thomas and whispered, "I crawled out through that window myself. Lucky we're so close to the ground. I'm not as young as I used to be." Miss

24

Rule gave a little laugh and covered her small mouth.

"That's wonderful, Edith. If only more teachers would follow their students sometimes. Then what did you do?"

"At first I didn't know what to do at all. There I was out of school in the middle of the afternoon with my students scattered in all directions. Then I decided. I walked straight around to the back of the school and cut across the soccer field and went home. I made myself a cup of tea and sat with my two cats on my lap and told them all about what happened. It may sound silly, William, for me to talk to cats, but they do listen."

"Not at all. I talk to my typewriter when I'm trying to write plays."

"Maybe today I'll be in trouble for leaving, but I had no students to teach. And it felt good to break the rules, if I say so myself."

Mr. Thomas laughed and clapped loudly at the end of JoAnn's performance. "Bravo! Miss Rule has come alive right before my eyes."

JoAnn's shoulders slumped and she let out her breath. Miss Rule was gone. "Thank you, sir."

3
Ottawa, here we come!

Patti was standing on the top step leaning against the railing at the school entrance. The baggy white shirt she wore outside her jeans made her body disappear, Alex noticed as he pushed the door open and walked outside. Her bulky blue sweater, rolled up at the sleeves, didn't help much either. Somewhere under all that shapeless clothing was a small body that looked great in gym shorts and a T-shirt. She also disguised her naturally curly hair with gel and spray to straighten it into short spikes over her forehead. But Alex didn't have to do much thinking to convince himself that she was looking good, as usual.

"Hi. Going home?" he asked, shifting his gym bag from one shoulder to the other and pushing it to rest across his back.

"Yeah. Soon as JoAnn gets here."

"I'll walk home with you." He hoped she caught the hidden meaning. It would be great to walk home with just Patti and not JoAnn too.

"Sure." She smiled, then her blue eyes were looking past him. "JoAnn! Over here!" she shouted.

JoAnn was dressed in the exact same outfit as Patti — baggy white shirt, jeans, and a blue sweater rolled at the sleeves. When they stood there together, they looked like an odd set of twins. Except that JoAnn was quite a bit taller than Patti.

"Alex is walking home with us," said Patti.

"Let's go then," JoAnn replied, starting down the school steps.

Alex moved over to the other side of Patti, shifting his gym bag again. There was barely enough room on the sidewalk for the three of them to walk comfortably.

"Did your father say you could go to Ottawa yet?" Patti asked.

"Not yet."

Carol was getting good at stage managing and it made Alex feel that his chances of going to Ottawa with the Drama Club were getting even more remote. Not many of the cast and crew talked about Carol learning Alex's job. Taboo. Except for Patti and JoAnn.

"I think you should just go," said JoAnn. "It's a school trip and it's not costing your father anything and you're underage for working anyway and maybe he could be arrested for making you work. Child abuse."

All Alex could do was give her a look. But she was rummaging through her pencil case and missed it.

"Mom says this trip'll be a real education, not like being in a classroom. And we'll see the Parliament buildings." Patti reached for the folded paper JoAnn had finally found.

"I've seen Parliament," Alex muttered.

"Trouble with your father is he doesn't know anything about plays. My parents take me to the theater all the time. They say it's a character-building experience," JoAnn said with a smug look.

Alex had an urge to reach out and rearrange the expression. He stifled it, holding back also on the compulsion to comment on how much JoAnn's character *needed* building too.

"Try telling your father you'll get better marks if he'll let you go," said Patti.

"You mean blackmail."

"Not really blackmail. Alex, you exaggerate so much. Just make a promise. He wants you to make high marks, doesn't he?"

"Or maybe he wants you to drop out and be a plumber just like him." JoAnn blinked once, as though realizing she'd gone too far this time.

Alex stopped. "I just remembered something I forgot at school. I gotta go back."

"I thought you were going to walk home with us."

"With you. I was going to walk home with you." He waited for JoAnn to open her big mouth and say something to that, but she didn't. "But I'll call you later," he added because, with all this about not going to Ottawa, he didn't need a fight with Patti too.

"I'll be at JoAnn's after supper."

"Why don't you call me when you get home, okay?" He was doing his best to act as if JoAnn wasn't standing there beside them at all.

Patti shrugged her shoulders. She might

even have pouted, although he could have been imagining that.

Alex walked across the boulevard and headed back toward school. Over his shoulder he watched Patti and JoAnn continue down the street, reading their note together. They were always writing notes in class, like they never had a chance to talk about anything. Then, when they were out of school, they read them over again. He was getting bored with it. He turned the corner and then doubled back two blocks, staying off the route the girls would take.

When he got home, he saw the van in front of the shop and all kinds of plumbing equipment scattered next to the open door. A clang brought his attention to where his father was, inside the van. He hadn't heard him approach, so Alex tried to sneak by unnoticed.

So far he had managed to postpone the inevitable news by staying out of his father's way. Ever since he'd come to listen in on the play, Alex had harbored a small hope that there was still a chance. He was afraid that soon his father would tell him once and for all that he couldn't go to Ottawa.

"That you?" The voice was muffled, but loud enough so it couldn't be avoided.

Alex stopped. "Yeah, it's me."

"Oh."

He waited in the quiet, expecting an order to come next: set the table, do your homework, pass me that wrench. But his father said nothing. Maybe he was concentrating on fitting something together. Usually he didn't talk when he was concentrating.

Dumbly, Alex stood there in the driveway.

Then the voice came again from the van, "I wanted to say something to you." And his father leaped down, wiping his hands with an old cloth.

"Yeah?" Cooperation was number one in Alex's mind. Ottawa was still on the map, he hoped.

"Mr. Thomas called me up today."

"He did?"

"Persistent son-of-a-gun."

Alex figured silence was the best answer at a time like this. Mr. Thomas was on his side, but his father was a stubborn person and, like a mule, he hated being pushed into anything. Ottawa could still fade *off* the map.

"So anyways, I told him you could go."

The shock of those words vibrated in Alex's eardrums and he wasn't sure that he'd heard correctly. This was too simple. Mr. Thomas makes a phone call and — *shazam!* Alex is on his way to Ottawa. There must be some kind of mistake.

"You mean I can go to Ottawa?"

"Where else? To the moon?" He stuffed the cloth into his back pocket and started to pile the plumbing supplies into the van. "Give me a hand with this."

"But — but — Dad. I — I mean — "

"Stop blubbering. It's only for three or four days."

"Four. And a half, if you count the night we go up there."

"But you gotta make up the time. I'll get

behind on those condominiums over on Beech Street."

"You mean I really can go? No kidding?" Alex was inside the van, stacking the hardware, taking stuff from his father almost automatically.

"That's what I said, isn't it?"

"But, why? I mean — "

"Why? If you're going to believe that Thomas, you'd think your whole life was wrapped up in that trip. He practically said he'd haul me in for neglect of my own son's education if I didn't let you go. No choice. But I told him" — Mr. MacInnis leaned across the box he'd rested on the bumper of the van and stared at Alex with a look that said it all — "I told him if there was any monkey business all hell'd break loose. If any son of mine's going off with a school trip, he'd better know that his father's still watching him." He let some silence underline his threat. "You get my meaning?"

"Sure, Dad. There won't be any problem."

For a few minutes Alex simply stacked the supplies as his father passed them to him. He didn't dare say anything else. Gradually the idea began to seem possible. Excitement started to crawl up Alex's arms and rush like slippery grass snakes across his shoulders. He could hardly breathe.

"That's the last," muttered his father. He sauntered into the workshop, leaving Alex staring, wondering if he'd just had a vivid daydream.

Some chrome faucets glinted from the dim shadows at the back of the van. A familiar clatter came from the workshop. *I told him you could go.* Those magic words floated up from Alex's memory. His father had actually said that.

"I told him you could go." He tried the words out himself.

Moving to the door of the van like a robot in slow-motion, he let the whole idea sink in. Then, with an explosive yelp, he jumped up and out.

* * *

The supper dishes were done and Alex had emptied the kitchen garbage can. He was restless. If his father asked him, right now, to wash the floor, he'd probably do it with a grin on his face.

Ottawa. Good old boss-of-the-country Ottawa.

He wanted to tell someone he would be going on the trip, but who could he tell? Patti was likely still at JoAnn's. Mr. Thomas already knew. No one else would care much one way or the other. Carol would be relieved, but he'd wait to tell her tomorrow.

Then it was almost eight-thirty. Patti still hadn't called, but he figured she must be home by now. He dialed her number.

"Hi, Patti. It's me and guess what. Dad says I can go!" Just hearing his voice saying those words out loud gave him a satisfaction he'd never thought would be his.

* * *

Alex could hear his father's mumbling in the bedroom down the hall and he knew he was struggling with a tie. For the rare occasions when a tie

32

was called for, he'd mutter and swear and call it a damned noose, or worse.

Alex headed in the direction of the mumbling. Walking into the bedroom, he saw a blue tie in midflight between the bureau where his father was standing and the wastebasket. It fell over the edge of the basket like a deflated snake.

"Almost ready, Dad?"

"I'm not wearing a tie." He slipped his shirt collar outside his sports jacket and ran his palm down the side of his hair.

"No one asked you to. Let's go." Before he turned to leave the room, Alex caught a glimpse of them both in the bureau mirror. He was looking at his father and his father was looking at him. They both seemed to be thinking how strange it was to be getting ready to go out together, even if it was just to a meeting at the school.

"No one's going to be dressed up," Alex said as they went downstairs. "It's only a meeting."

When they got to the school, there were a few cars lined up by the doors where, in the daytime, no cars were allowed to park. Some kids on bikes were doing figure eights on the school grounds and showing off with a few wheelies.

Soon Mr. Thomas stood at the front of the room, trying to make the formal meeting seem informal. He leaned one hand against a chair and stuffed the other into his pants pocket. He talked about the privilege of the trip and about how he'd look out for the students as if they were his own children.

One of the boys called out, "Daddy!" and that got a few laughs.

Then he passed around sheets of paper with the rules for the trip. People cleared their throats and read the document with care. There were rules about such things as curfews and respect for property, and at the end, a paragraph about representing the school in another province.

"Even if we don't win the competition, we must always show the best side of ourselves," Mr. Thomas said to end his speech. "Any questions?"

One woman raised her hand. "Mr. Thomas, I appreciate all the work you're doing for our children." Short applause. "And I certainly don't mean to be negative by bringing up this subject — but teenagers will be teenagers." Her daughter, sitting beside her, slouched. "If by any chance someone in your group does not follow the rules, what will be your course of action?"

"It would depend, of course, on which rule and on the circumstances." Mr. Thomas pinched the end of his chin. "Our play needs all its cast and crew, so I would try my best to take a course of action that wouldn't interfere with the rehearsals or with the final performance of the play itself. However," he added, pausing to look meaningfully around at all the students, "if we should run into undue difficulty, then I'd have no recourse but to send that person, or those persons, home on a direct flight. I would phone the parents to ask them to wire airfare and meet their son or daughter at the airport."

You could almost hear the students gulp in astonishment.

34

"But that's an extreme measure and one I do not foresee being taken. We've worked too hard to get this far and then blow our chances at the festival. Am I right?"

The students stomped their feet and cheered, as if they'd already won, or as if to dispel any thoughts of being sent home.

Coffee and donuts were served after the meeting. Parents and club members mingled, talking about the play, about Ottawa, about the weather, about how the Blue Jays might do this year. Alex's father defended the high cost of plumbing about three times, once to a woman who told a joke about the surgeon who quit his job to take up plumbing because he could charge more.

Outside in the parking lot the sky had darkened to a deep navy blue. The kids on the bikes had gone home.

As they pulled out of the schoolyard, Alex's father seemed to be concentrating on something. Alex hoped whatever it was, he wouldn't want to talk about it. It looked serious. Although the permission letter had been signed and the medical form filled out saying Alex wouldn't be a health hazard, he knew he still had a fragile hold on the trip to Ottawa.

"Now those rules aren't a joke." Mr. MacInnis's voice was stern.

"Huh?"

"That sheet of rules we got back there. That's serious and you got to follow them, to the letter." He stressed the last three words as though he was quoting the Bible.

"I know, Dad. I will." Alex was treading on thin ice.

"I mean it," reiterated his father.

"I do too, Dad."

"And don't bother coming home if you get up to no good up there."

"Gee, Dad, you act like I got some kind of plan to get in trouble or something." It was frustrating having to defend himself when he wouldn't even think about doing anything wrong. How could a guy win?

"Just so you know."

They drove along in silence. Alex thought about the week and a half left before the plane took off and he'd be safely belted into his seat. Until that time, he knew, he'd have to be so good his brain would squeak from all the clean thoughts. He'd work for his father, never miss homework, and be on time for school. This would be the straightest nine days of his life!

4

Double trouble

Alex put his headphones down and grinned. That was good. More than good! It was the slickest rehearsal they'd had. Even better than back home.

"Take an hour for lunch," shouted Mr. Thomas. "Be back in the conference room at exactly 1:10 and we'll hear any gripes you have and make some plans for seeing Parliament tomorrow."

Everyone dispersed in clumps and clusters.

"Meet you in the lobby," said Alex to Patti as she and JoAnn headed for the dressing room.

"In about ten."

After he'd double-checked to see that he'd switched the panel off, Alex sat alone on the set. The schoolroom looked gray and bare and sur-real, now, without Miss Rule and all the students. It was a flat painting with no sounds and no lights and no lines to bring it to life. He tapped his headphones in a kind of reminder to himself of the power he had as stage manager. Even Mr. Thomas, sitting out there in the back row, gave up authority when the house lights went down and the stage lights illuminated the world of their play.

The students on stage knew that when they reached into their desk drawers, on cue, for that pen or that dictionary, it would be there. Alex would've made sure. And when Grace opened the window and the first sounds of outdoors were let into the stifling classroom, there'd be the birds chirping and whistling. It was power, no doubt about that.

He was feeling good. Throwing his jacket over his shoulder, Alex headed to the men's washroom near the backstage entrance.

He pushed open the door and stopped. "Hi," he said, more out of surprise than friendliness. What else do you say to a guy standing in the john reading a book like he was in front of the public library waiting for a bus?

"How's it going?" said the bookworm, hardly lifting his goggled eyes from the book. The cover looked familiar to Alex, but he wasn't about to stare.

As Alex unzipped his fly, the bookworm turned a page. It wasn't easy to ignore the fact that a guy was reading just a couple meters away. In a washroom, for crying out loud! There's weird and there's really weird, thought Alex.

But then the bookworm lifted himself away from the wall and said, "You in one of the plays?"

"Stage manager," said Alex.

"Complicated job."

"Yeah." The men's washroom seemed an inappropriate place to philosophize on the duties of a stage manager.

"Well, see ya."

"Right," said the bookworm.

Just by chance Alex caught a closer look at the cover of the book the guy was reading. *Lord of the Flies*. Some of the grade elevens were reading that. But, too late, he knew he'd given the bookworm something else to talk about.

"You ever read this?"

"Naw. Just seen it around," he replied, trying to sound uninterested.

"The guys in this book're weird."

Alex thought his mind had just been read.

"They take over this island and set up their own government and make these vicious rules and turn some guys into outlaws and some guys into vigilantes. The guy who wrote it got a Nobel prize."

"Yeah. Well, I gotta go. Patti's waiting and —"

"Sure. See you around." And he went back to his novel as if Alex were just stepping on a bus headed in another direction.

"What took you so long?" Patti asked as Alex joined her and JoAnn.

"Had to double-check some things on the set," he said. There was no way he was about to describe the encounter in the washroom. "Let's get to the cafeteria. I'm famished."

* * *

At the morning meeting with Mr. Thomas, final arrangements were made for the Drama Club to visit the Parliament buildings later that afternoon. Although the elected representatives had recessed, Mr. Thomas insisted it would still be worth having a look. "This is where the great decisions of our nation are made — and the not-so-great ones too," he joked. The next few hours would be left for people to do their own thing.

Alex had already turned the handle of the door before he realized that he should have gone to a different washroom. Too late. And there, leaning on the radiator, continuing *Lord of the Flies* like he'd never even left the day before, was the bookworm.

"Hi."

"Hi."

This was getting ridiculous.

"How're rehearsals going?"

"Pretty good."

"I've been watching some of them. B.C.'s got a not-bad play. You from B.C.?"

"Nova Scotia."

"East."

"Down east," Alex agreed. He'd heard some guys from Toronto saying that as if Nova Scotia were off the map.

"You like grass?"

The sudden switch of topic threw Alex off a bit. "I do it sometimes," he lied. An image appeared in his mind of his father raving about how druggies were taking over the shopping centers. No point admitting, though, that he'd never dared try the stuff.

"I got some. Not like the stuff you get off the street. That junk's so messed up with herbal tea you don't know whether you should smoke it or serve it in a china cup to your great aunt. This is pure. Canadian Gold. Grew it myself."

Alex just listened.

"Tell you what. I'll give you a joint. Gratis. If you like the stuff, I'll get you some more tomorrow."

"Well, it's kinda — wouldn't it be kinda risky?"

"No problem," he said. "I can show you a safe place to smoke it. Trust me. What have you got to lose?"

"We're in the middle of a rehearsal," Alex lied.

"I'll hang around till it's over. I got all kinds of time."

Alex was beginning to feel pressured. "Someone pay you to sell this stuff?" he asked.

"Hold it. I don't push. I offer. You don't want it, I don't push."

"It's just not every day you come into a washroom and find a guy reading like it was a library and then he says he's selling grass."

"My name is Benjamin Holbrook. What's yours?" He held out his hand as if a formal handshake would make everything normal.

"Alex MacInnis."

"Well, Alex, like I said, I got this Canadian Gold. Pure. My grandparents are stuck with me every summer while Mom and Dad do Europe, and they've got a farm they don't do much with. So I've got a patch of field way in back of the house where it's sunny all day and my special grass grows in among some tomato plants. This year my crop is going to be even better than last."

He placed his hand on Alex's shoulder like they were business partners.

"Aren't you afraid you'll get caught? Someone's going to see your field."

"No one on that back road knows what grass looks like unless it's rolled up in white paper pinched at both ends and hanging from the fingers of a drippy-eyed kid in an alley. I tell you I'm safe."

The door suddenly opened and a janitor shuffled in with an armload of toilet paper.

"Come on and I'll show you that book I said I'd lend you," Benjamin continued casually, guiding Alex out of the washroom.

"Hey," Alex said as soon as they were in the hall, "I had to use the facilities."

"Later," insisted Benjamin, gently pushing him down the corridor and into the first room on the left. "I'm telling you, this stuff is worth the price of admission. Not that I'm charging you for this first toke."

They were in a room piled precariously with stage props and costumes and half-painted flats. Benjamin had obviously been there before. "Take a seat." He pointed to a wooden crate, then dug in his pockets for matches and a joint rolled as thick as the index finger of a basketball player.

Alex got even more nervous. "Look," he said with a gust of too much confidence, "I gotta go. I told Patti I'd be right back. Besides, I can't take this stuff and run the play." That excuse sounded pretty good, he had to admit.

Benjamin held the joint and the unlit match suspended in front of his face, considering the situation. Alex wanted to squirm but didn't. "Right. You're right. Timing's off. You know where you can find me, buddy. Bring your girlfriend, if you want."

"Into the men's john?"

"Ha!" laughed Benjamin as if Alex were the best comedian this side of New York.

Alex turned to go. "Well, see ya." He smiled, but it was a phony smile.

While Alex was thinking he'd find another washroom next time, Benjamin was thinking how much Alex would like the Canadian Gold if he ever tried it.

* * *

The street mall was swarming with shoppers. Some elderly ladies were easing the pressure on their feet by sitting on benches circling tall trees.

JoAnn, Patti and Alex entered a small crafts store. They strolled around displays of bracelets made from pewter and silver, brushed past some handwoven scarves and ponchos, and finally stopped at a counter where dozens of earrings hung on a carousel.

"May I help you?" asked a gray-haired salesclerk politely.

Patti was holding a pair of gold chain earrings against her ear, showing Alex.

"Sure," said JoAnn smoothly. "I want to buy a souvenir for my mother. I'm here in Ottawa at a drama festival."

"Well, isn't that nice. Let's see." She held up a pair of dangling silver earrings. "These are fifteen dollars. Would that be in your price range?"

"Oh yes, that's not too expensive," cooed JoAnn. "But my mom doesn't have pierced ears, so —"

"We'll just look through these others then," replied the salesclerk.

"Do you have anything with a small pink stone?" asked JoAnn.

Patti leaned over her shoulder. Alex was engrossed in a nearby display of brightly colored watches.

"Let me see." The woman pulled open a large drawer under the counter and started rummaging in it. Emerging, finally, she said, "No pink, but these have a delicate white stone. Your mother could wear them with anything."

"Hm," said JoAnn, studying them carefully. "I don't know."

"I like them," said Patti. The stone was like a frozen raindrop in the center of a silver circle.

"No. I think Mom has a pair something like that already. They're pretty, but —"

"Perhaps we have something else."

"Well, I think I'll just keep looking. I'll come back if I can't find what I want. Thank you," JoAnn said.

"We're going now, Alex," shouted Patti.

"Okay. Wait for me outside. I'll just be a couple of minutes."

"Let's sit over there," said JoAnn. A woman with three bulky shopping bags was just getting up from a bench outside the shop.

44

When they were alone, JoAnn opened her palm to show two glittering silver loop earrings.

Patti's mouth dropped open. "What —"

"I just took them. When the clerk went looking for the pink stones."

"But — I mean, what if —" Shock prevented Patti from completing that thought.

"It was easy. Like acting. You just pretend you're looking and you say things and make it look real."

"But it's crazy, JoAnn!"

"It's not!" she retorted. "Oh come on, Patti. You try it. Just once."

Patti looked down at the silver earrings. "I'd get caught. I know I would."

"No you wouldn't. All you have to do is make sure no one sees you. I'll be there to distract people."

"I just can't. It's too risky. I can't act like you can. Besides, Alex'll be right there too and —"

"Okay, okay. But it's no big sweat. Honest."

"JoAnn? Are you going to do it again?"

"Maybe."

"Even if Alex is right there?"

"Sure. Why not?"

"He might see you do it."

"He won't."

"What if someone else sees you? Remember that meeting we had with Mr. Thomas and our parents? If anyone breaks the rules on this trip they'll be sent home, he said. He meant it too, and that was just for breaking curfew or having a party in one of the rooms or stuff like that. If you get caught shoplifting —"

45

"Shh. Here comes Alex."

"You guys get anything?" he asked.

"No," said Patti.

"Yeah," said JoAnn at the same time. "I got some earrings for Mom."

"Almost bought one of those watches. Maybe I will if I still have enough money left by Friday."

"Let's go back to the dorm," Patti said with a fake yawn. "I'm getting tired."

"Not yet. I want to check out that department store," said JoAnn.

"I think it'll be raining soon," Patti argued. Gray clouds were floating threateningly above them.

"What's a little rain?"

Reluctantly Patti agreed and the three headed across the street.

When they left the department store, JoAnn boldly carried a glaring yellow and blue striped umbrella. She had picked it out moments after they'd entered the store, carrying it with her from one floor to the next as though she'd left home prepared for the inevitable rain. Patti had seen her take it. Luckily, though, Alex had headed down a different aisle.

Just outside the door JoAnn stopped to put up the umbrella, although only a few intermittent drops were falling. Under it they made their way back to the dorm to get ready for their afternoon tour of the Parliament buildings.

5
Protest

It wasn't far to walk to Parliament Hill, but it was still raining. JoAnn and Patti were together under the large umbrella, and drips kept sneaking down Alex's neck from the edge as he walked along beside Patti.

When the group got to the eternal flame, Mr. Thomas stopped them to give a speech about how it was first lit in 1967 during Canada's 100th birthday. Someone wanted to know why the rain didn't smother the flames and someone else wanted to know if it ever went out accidentally. But Alex wasn't listening because a tent and what looked like some clowns at one corner of the lawns had caught his attention.

"Sir," he interrupted, "what's going on there where that tent is? Is it an outdoor theater?"

Mr. Thomas looked over the heads of the cluster of students around him and studied the situation. "No, Alex. It's a protest group that's been in the news for months now. They're fighting the U.S. testing of the cruise missile in Canada. Let's go take a closer look."

The grass around the tent was flat and dull compared with the rest of the lush green lawns.

Inside the small tent were a few chairs, two cots, and a camper stove with a blackened kettle. It wasn't quite furnished to give the impression of a vacation camping trip, but it didn't look like a war zone either, Alex noticed.

The protesters, though, gave him a weird, shivery feeling. Their faces were painted white, like mime players, and they had gray, exaggerated frowns with large black tears dripping down their cheeks. There were about seven or eight of them standing or sitting, ignoring the drizzling rain, each with the same painted expression of misery. Everything they wore was black. It made Alex think of the end of the world.

"Excuse me," said Mr. Thomas. "Is there a spokesperson for your group? Some students here have questions about the testing of the cruise missile."

A protester showed them large black and white pictures framed in metal and suspended on a pole. Heavy plastic coated the pages. In the photographs the missile looked like a toy. There were ordinary small towns and leafy trees. Dubbed in on the scene was a short cigar-shaped cruise missile with small wings skimming down the main drag like some kind of futuristic automobile. One of the protesters outlined the facts: how fast, how far, how low, how much money to build, how many people to burn.

"But why should we be so bugged about testing a blank bomb?" asked one of the students.

The protester lifted the heavy pages to the very last one. "The bombs won't always be blank," she said simply.

The picture on the last page did not look like the earth at all. Way in the background could be seen a line of gray mountains against a steel sky. A few skeleton trees poked up out of the scoured earth. Even the rubble of what must have been buildings was raked to smoothness. "This is Hiroshima." There were no streets and no homes and no sign of where people would have passed by.

"Do you feel that what you're doing is effective?" asked Mr. Thomas.

"Doing something is more effective than doing nothing."

A few students shuffled restlessly and Mr. Thomas got the hint. He thanked the protester for the talk and shook her hand energetically, wishing her luck and saying something about writing to his Member of Parliament as soon as he got back home. Alex silently made a bet with himself that Thomas would make the whole class do that as some kind of English project. Thirty-two letters dumped on some guy's desk to ruin his day.

Just as he turned to leave, one of the protesters, smaller than the others, came over and put his hand on Alex's shoulder. His face didn't show any expression other than the painted one. "How's the play coming?"

"Huh?" The voice sounded a bit familiar, but how could one of these protesters know about the play? "Uh — it's not bad."

"It's me. Benjamin."

Standing in front of him was the washroom pusher. Alex was stunned, and for a minute couldn't say a thing.

"Close your mouth or a cruise will track through it." Benjamin didn't even smile at his own joke.

"What are you doing here?"

"Same as everyone else."

"But — "

"What did you think? That I live in washrooms selling grass? Well, I don't."

"I know that, but — well — I just didn't think you'd care much about things like this, if you know what I mean."

"Grass doesn't compare with the cruise."

From the distance came a shout from Patti.

"Come back after the tour. Stay a while. See what it's like here, if you want," offered Benjamin.

"Sure. Yeah. I'll come back maybe." And he turned away, still trying to figure things out. Why was Benjamin being so nice to him? It wasn't as if he'd dare try to sell the dope right there in front of the Parliament buildings. Or would he?

Standing in the gallery of the House, Alex couldn't get Benjamin and the protesters out of his mind. There they were, out on the lawn and had been for months, while inside all was polished and velvet and official.

There were carved wooden seats on either side of the room and a throne at the front. People stood up here to argue issues. Others replied with thumping on desks and hooting. Alex had seen that on television lots of times. He wondered from which seat the first person had risen to say they should test the cruise, and where the arguments against came from. Then he thought of Benjamin's Canadian Gold. It was weird to picture this huge official place full of people making laws about grass. Maybe they even talked about it on the same day as they discussed the cruise missile.

"Sir! Mr. Thomas!" Alex brushed past the other students as they gathered back at the entrance doors. "Sir, would it be okay with you if I went back over to where those protesters are? I can find my own way back to the dorm."

"Sure. I guess there's no harm in that. Captured your curiosity, did they?"

"Sort of. Anyway, I won't stay long."

"Won't stay long where?" Patti and JoAnn had caught up. JoAnn was struggling with the umbrella, even though it had stopped raining. With a *whoosh*, it opened up.

"I'm just going to check out those cruise protesters again." Then to JoAnn he added sarcastically, "If you'd come out from under that thing for a few seconds you'd find out it isn't raining anymore."

"I just like it, okay? What's it to you?"

"What're you going back there for?" asked Patti.

Alex didn't answer. Lately JoAnn was getting to him, especially on this trip. Things like that umbrella were such a big deal. Just a plain umbrella you could buy anywhere. It seemed the only way to avoid JoAnn would be not hanging out with Patti.

"I'll wait by the cafeteria door at dinner

51

time." He was looking directly at Patti, trying to freeze out JoAnn. But it didn't work.

"Okay," she said unenthusiastically. "We'll be there around five-thirty." And the two girls walked away under the yellow and blue umbrella.

Benjamin saw Alex coming across the path and got up from the canvas chair where he'd been sitting next to two other protesters. "This is the guy I told you about. Hey, Alex, meet Paul and Estella. They organized this whole thing. This is Alex."

Handshakes and nods were exchanged, but no smiles. Alex figured it must be the first rule: *No smiles while on protest duty!*

"I told them you're from Nova Scotia. And about the play. You're one of us, in a way. You'd fit right in here."

Alex wasn't quite getting the drift of what Benjamin was hinting at.

"If you're interested," said Estella, "we've got lots of black shirts and make-up. We can use all the bodies we can recruit. It's almost like acting in a play, except you need to be ready to answer questions."

"Hold it," answered Alex, feeling slightly cornered again, as he had in the washroom when Benjamin had first offered him the grass. "I don't know what Benjamin told you, but I'm no actor. I'm the stage manager and —"

"If you're interested in banning the cruise," interrupted Paul, "that's all we need."

"Come on, Alex," said Benjamin, with just

the hint of a grin sneaking through his painted frown. "What's to lose?"

"I don't know anything about the cruise." Alex was becoming exasperated, but no one seemed to notice.

"Benjamin will fill you in while I put on the make-up," said Paul.

And before he could analyze what he was getting into, he was sitting on a canvas chair in the tent with Paul applying a slippery cream base to his face. Benjamin flipped through a book and crammed Alex with enough information about the cruise missile to make him an instant expert.

Alex felt strange. The make-up was thick on his face, and his eyebrows, blackened with a charcoal pencil, itched. His hair was stuffed under a smooth cap which fitted like skin over his skull. The black T-shirt was a bit too big, but Paul rolled up the sleeves and slipped the white gloves up over them.

"Check yourself out," said Benjamin, holding up a cracked mirror.

A sad white face stared out from it. At the edge of the white cheek a blackened tear hung ready to slide down. With the cap and the make-up and the black turtleneck, nothing of the real Alex showed through.

"Stick out your tongue," said Benjamin.

He did and saw a fleshy pink roll break through the painted frown. It made Alex laugh and his teeth, though perfectly even and white, looked yellow and inhuman in contrast with the stark white make-up.

"Now you know why we don't smile when we're outside this tent. It'd scare everyone away." Benjamin grinned for the first time, which made Paul and Alex laugh too.

"Let's go." Paul wiped his hands and led the way out of the tent.

What am I doing here? Alex asked himself silently. But somehow it felt right — sticky make-up, yellow teeth and all. Even Benjamin, the washroom pusher.

Benjamin was close behind when Alex heard the scream. Then suddenly something smacked against the flap of the tent right next to him, splashing his face. The whole protest group burst into action, moving, ducking and shouting. Someone grabbed his arm and pushed him down on the grass. His heart was pounding as the hollering grew louder.

Above the noise he heard Estella ordering people into the tent. Benjamin started to crawl backwards. "Come on, Alex!"

All Alex could think of were war movies — trenches and enemy fire and crawling along the ground on your belly. He lifted his head from the grass, leaving a smudge of white where he'd been pressing so hard. Exactly what was happening? What had hit the tent? Why was everyone taking cover?

Just then he had his answer. Out of the corner of his eye, a split-second before it hit, Alex caught sight of something white. There was a sharp pain as it shattered against his forehead. Something cool and gooey oozed down his cheek. He reached up to feel his face. Bright yellow and

54

transparent white smeared the fingertips of his gloves. Eggs. The enemy was throwing eggs.

Even before all the protesters were back in the tent, two mounties on horseback came to the rescue. The egg-throwers scattered.

The red-uniformed men dismounted, holding the reins of their horses and surveying the mess around the tent. Chairs were overturned and the large picture book was on the ground. Egg shells were scattered everywhere. Yolk stained the tent and the grass. Some of the protesters were covered with large sticky patches.

"Want some help with this?" one of them asked.

"We'll get to it. Right now, we've got ourselves an audience," said Estella.

No one even bothered cleaning the guck off themselves as the crowds gathered closer around the tent. People seemed more interested in the egg fight than the cruise, Alex observed, but Paul and the others ignored that minor detail. The picture book was put to work and small clusters of the curious got lessons on the cruise.

"That was a close one," said Benjamin, inspecting the spot where the egg had hit Alex. "Does it hurt?" He reached up to touch Alex's head.

"Ow!"

"It cut a hole right through the cap. Lucky it wasn't a bit lower or it would've sliced your forehead. No damage. Come on, let's get to work."

Benjamin approached three guys a year or two older than himself. They didn't look the least bit interested in the cruise.

Alex wiped some egg from the side of his face onto his sleeve.

"We're here as a protest against the cruise," said Benjamin simply. "Canada's agreement to test — "

"Only one kinda cruise I know about," interrupted one of the guys. He laughed loudly and the others joined in. "All I can see here is a bunch of clowns lookin' like idiots." His voice had a hint of violence in it.

"The cruise missile is a low-altitude bomb which can track through — "

"Save it, nerd," said the same guy. He folded his arms across his chest.

So did Benjamin. For a moment they both stood as if considering the next move.

Alex thought about his room back at the dorm.

"You don't fool us. You guys are Commies," said the leader. "You just wanna stop the testing so the Commies can take over."

"Right," said Benjamin. But only Alex caught his sarcasm.

"When you wipe off those clown faces today, we'll be waiting for you. Both of you." And he turned and walked away. The other two guys followed.

"You win some, you lose some." Benjamin began to search out other bystanders to lecture to. Alex followed, wondering whether Benjamin was mildly dense or just plain crazy to have faced those guys like that. And what if they really meant what they said about waiting for them?

An elderly couple listened intently to Benjamin, who did a terrific job of embellishing his lecture with scenes of grandchildren and gardens and the low-tracking cruise. Throughout the whole thing Alex was forced to stand perfectly still while the lady dabbed and rubbed at his forehead and cheek with a small handkerchief bordered with violet lace.

After the couple left, Benjamin turned to Alex. "Back to the tent," he ordered. "You've only got half a face."

In the cracked mirror Alex could see how efficiently the lady had been with her lace handkerchief. Through the white and black make-up emerged part of the real Alex.

"May as well both take our make-up off," said Benjamin, scooping out a handful of make-up remover and applying it to his own face. He passed the large crock to Alex. "I've got to catch a bus."

"Where to?"

"My grandparents."

Alex pictured green fields with a little white house on a hill and a large red barn out back. Behind the barn, at the bottom of the hill, tucked in near some woods, would be a patch of tomato plants with rows and rows of tiny marijuana shoots growing neatly among them. The Canadian Gold.

Benjamin had put on his pullover and was combing his hair. As soon as he had it in place, he took both hands and ruffled it again, enough to take away the just-combed look. He took his glasses from a shelf. "Now I can see again," he grinned. "Did I miss any excitement out there?"

Alex grinned back. It was hard not to like this guy, he thought to himself. He's different, that's for sure.

"Do you think we should tell someone about those guys?" he asked. "Maybe Paul?"

"Those losers left ages ago. They're all talk."

Outside the tent, Benjamin turned to Alex. "I'll be around the festival tonight. Might see you."

"Sure."

Yet Alex was confused. He did want to meet up with Benjamin later. Sounded like a lot more fun than trailing around with Patti and JoAnn and their umbrella. But the festival was probably all business for Benjamin. He'd be spending his time in the washroom, very likely. If he got mixed up in that, Alex knew, it would only mean trouble. Maybe he should just lie low tonight and avoid any contact with Benjamin at all.

As he and Benjamin moved out onto the street, the three guys who had threatened them appeared directly in front of them, grinning but not the least bit friendly.

"Commies," one guy growled.

"Do you even know what a Communist is?" Alex just about passed out when he heard the question.

The answer Benjamin got was a fist just about at belt level. A second guy moved fast and Alex felt a feeble punch in his shoulder. Before he could get control of his balance, a second punch landed square in his jaw. He toppled. Someone screamed. He saw a black sneaker swing into Benjamin's shin and heard him yelp and fall.

Another shout and then lots of pairs of feet were getting in a few good kicks before the three guys sensed their time limit and took off.

A man was helping Benjamin up and Alex leaned into a woman's arms. His tooth felt loose and some blood dripped across his lip.

"You all right?" asked Benjamin, even before he was on his feet.

"I don't know." It was the truth.

In seconds they heard the wail of a police siren followed by the screech of brakes nearby. Two policemen rushed toward the crowd that had gathered. The man who'd helped Benjamin gave details of what he'd seen, and one policeman took off running down the street. Soon he was back, discouraged. "Nothing."

"You kids know those guys?"

"Yes and no," said Benjamin. And then he explained the scenario.

"We'll take you to the station. Just for a few more questions."

As they eased their way into the back seat of the cruiser, Benjamin was thinking about a certain problem he had with one of the three troublemakers, while Alex was trying to reassure himself that just because a guy was being taken to a police station didn't necessarily mean he was in trouble.

6

Police station blues

At the police station Benjamin and Alex were shown into a small room. To their surprise it didn't have a naked lightbulb dangling from a single overhead wire, nor did it have hard wooden chairs and blank gray walls. Instead there were some easy chairs, a coffee table with magazines, and pictures on the walls.

Yet they were both nervous. Maybe it had something to do with the man standing at the front desk handcuffed to a policeman, or maybe it was all the computers and the uniforms in the radio dispatch room they'd passed.

"Why don't you fellas relax a little here while the sergeant gets organized to ask a few questions?" It obviously wasn't the first time the policeman had seen guys squirm in this room. "Can I get you a can of pop?"

"Sure," said Benjamin, and Alex quickly agreed.

Benjamin's brain was working like mad trying to come up with a plan to avoid having to face the one mugger again. And only he knew the reason why.

When the policeman returned with the pop,

he was accompanied by a sergeant and the questioning began. The story was a short one.

"And you don't recall ever seeing them before?"

"No," said Benjamin quickly.

"We'll have to get in touch with your parents — " He paused to check the data sheet they'd filled out when they first got to the station. "Your guardians, that is — Mr. Thomas for you, Alex, and your grandparents, Benjamin. We'll have to ask them to come to the station."

Alex shifted uneasily in his seat. He wasn't exactly thrilled with the idea of making Mr. Thomas come to a police station. Benjamin didn't look too pleased either. When his parents called every Sunday night from wherever they were in Europe, they expected to chat about safe things like the weather, not visits to police stations. But they had no choice. While the sergeant went to arrange the calls, the two boys settled back to wait, trying not to think.

"Seems you guys are pretty much up on this cruise business," said the sergeant when he came back into the room. "Nice to see. A lot of kids your age are just cruisin' for trouble." He guffawed at his own joke and Benjamin and Alex tried to join in. "I'll tell you, in my business I get the wrong side of kids. The trouble side — drugs mostly."

Alex sipped his pop and didn't dare look in Benjamin's direction.

"But with guys like you two," continued the sergeant, "maybe there's hope. Even most adults don't take the time to find out about the cruise or

61

anything else. When did you get mixed up in all this?" He was looking at Benjamin.

"Oh I dunno, a couple months ago. I saw the protest on TV and figured I'd join, since I have a lot of time to kill after school."

The sergeant was surprised. "You mean it's like some kind of hobby?"

"Sort of."

"I don't buy it," he said. "Lots of other hobbies for kids these days."

Benjamin concentrated on the can of pop in his hand. Some things you just didn't talk about. It was too hard to explain. One night you're home alone watching TV and a warning about parental guidance flashes on the screen. Nobody's around to say no, so you watch the end of the world — a nuclear attack. And this one man in the movie, when he knows it's going to happen, keeps driving and driving to get as far away as he can. People are holed up in their basements and food is running out. Someone shoots a guy for trespassing. Only burnt out, blank, wasted ground, for crying out loud!

Sitting there alone in his parents' comfortable living room, picturing that kind of alone, Benjamin had decided that if he ever knew a bomb was going to hit he'd drive like hell toward it, not away. Oblivion. Sweet escape.

Then the protesters were there on the screen saying no to the whole thing. Benjamin had figured that had to be better than driving toward a direct hit.

"And how about you?" the sergeant asked

Alex. "All the way up here for a drama festival and suddenly you're a cruise protester."

"It was sort of an accident," he said.

"I get the hint. Mind my own business. But all the same, I gotta admire you kids." He drained the last of his coffee and looked at his watch.

Just then the door opened. A policeman looked in and said, "Could I see you out in the hall, sergeant?"

When he came back into the room, the sergeant had a wide grin on his face. "Well, boys, looks like we've got your friends. Seems there was a witness who noticed which way they ran. We caught one of them and the rest was easy. Now all we need from you two is positive identification."

The door opened again and a small, elderly woman in a navy blue suit hurried into the room. "Benjamin. Thank goodness you're all right. He's fine," she said to the gray-haired man who came in behind her, supporting himself on a polished wooden cane. "You *are* fine, aren't you Benjamin?" she asked nervously.

"Sure, Gran. Just a few aches in my stomach, that's all." He gave her a hug. "Alex, these are my grandparents, Mr. and Mrs. Holbrook. This is Alex MacInnis. He's from Nova Scotia."

Alex went over to shake hands with Benjamin's grandfather. Then Mr. Thomas was in the room too.

"Hi, sir." Alex couldn't wipe out the feeling that somehow he'd messed things up for the whole Drama Club. He felt guilty. "Uh — sorry, sir."

"Nothing to be sorry about. You weren't in the wrong." He placed his hand on Alex's shoulder.

After introductions all around, the sergeant asked everyone to have a seat. As the police officer talked, Benjamin kept thinking about having to identify the three thugs. What he hadn't told anyone yet was that he had met one of them barely a week ago during a deal. The guy hadn't recognized Benjamin with his face covered in white make-up, and later he'd been too busy with the fight.

It would be okay if the police used those one-way mirrors or a stage lineup where the victims couldn't be seen by the criminals. But maybe that only happened in movies.

"So," the sergeant was saying, "that's all that's left to do."

Benjamin had been only half listening, but he knew what was coming. The sergeant got up. "We'll bring the boys back in about five minutes," he said to Mr. Thomas and Benjamin's grandparents. "Just wait here, please."

No mirror and no stage lineup separated Benjamin and Alex from the boys they were asked to identify.

"Let's get right to the point," said the sergeant. "Are these the ones who assaulted you today?"

"They sure are," said Alex. The tallest one gave him a look that was almost a snarl.

"Yes, sir," said Benjamin quietly. He tried to

make his statement brief so he could get out of the room fast.

"You're certain?"

Why does he have to be so thorough? thought Benjamin, feeling time ticking away like a bomb. He was desperate to escape the critical gaze of the guy who'd bought the joints from him. Already he'd squinted twice in Benjamin's direction.

"Thank you, boys. That's all. We'll prepare the statements for you to sign."

Trying to appear casual, Benjamin strolled toward the door. *Tick. Tick. Tick.* Maybe he did have time.

The sergeant was opening the door for them. Alex was the first to get there, and it would have looked too suspicious for Benjamin to elbow him out of the way and rush past, although that's what he felt like doing. *Tick. Tick. Tick.* Almost there.

But, as though someone had pinched him, the guy sat up suddenly and practically shouted, "Hey! I know that dude!" He was looking directly at Benjamin, who looked around innocently. "He's a pusher!" The time bomb had exploded.

Alex froze his face in what he hoped was a shocked expression.

"I'm telling you, he's a pusher!"

"A commie clown pusher?" said Benjamin coolly, baiting the guy.

Boy, thought Alex, Benjamin sure knew how to react fast.

"I suppose you bought lots of stuff from me. Or maybe you guys attacked us because you were cleaning up the streets. Good try."

65

"I'm telling you, he's a pusher! I — " The guy looked desperately around, first at his friends, then at the sergeant and Benjamin.

"So should we also question you about some kind of drug deal you've been in on?" asked the sergeant.

The guy quickly realized he was cornered. He slumped down and shut up, fuming. Alex noticed that Benjamin was enjoying it.

Back in the other room everyone was smiling. The ordeal was over. Now, Alex felt, the Drama Club was off the hook. Benjamin was starting to relax as well. What a close call!

Mr. Thomas asked the sergeant if that was the end of the identification process. "This's the last you need to see of the inside of this place," the sergeant assured him.

"I have a wonderful idea!" Mrs. Holbrook said, stopping in the hallway. "Let's all go back to the farm and have a nice dinner together. Would you join us, Alex? Mr. Thomas? We would be just delighted if you came."

"Sounds cool," said Benjamin as he edged toward the door. He wanted to get out of the police station as quickly as possible.

"Thank you, Mrs. Holbrook," said Mr. Thomas, "but I'll have to decline. There are eleven students waiting for me back at the dorm. But I don't see why Alex can't go along."

"Thanks, sir. I'd like that." The thought of missing a cafeteria meal was a small miracle in itself.

"We'll drive Alex back before it gets too

late," said Mrs. Holbrook, as they parted from Mr. Thomas in the parking lot.

"No worry. I know he'll be safe and sound."

7

If you're good, you can chew gum on Fridays

Mrs. Holbrook parked the Mercedes in front of the garage.

The farmhouse didn't seem like a farmhouse at all. No chickens clucked around the veranda and there was no barn behind, sheltering pigs and horses and cows. They didn't even have a pet cat, as far as Alex could tell.

Benjamin held the front door open for his grandfather, who lifted his legs from one step to another as if they were as wooden as his cane. Once inside, Mrs. Holbrook helped him off with his coat and settled him into a chair in the den with a blanket across his knees.

"Now you just rest here while I see what Mary's planning for dinner."

Alex was looking around trying to take in everything at once. The hallway they had come through was hung with paintings and had a wide, carpeted stairway curving up to the second floor. The den was filled with hundreds of hardcover books and had a huge desk in the middle. It didn't take much imagination to realize that the meaning of all this was money.

"Take your friend up and show him your room, Benjamin. It'll be some time before dinner," said Mrs. Holbrook. She brushed her fingertips lightly against a small bruise on his cheek. "Those hoodlums," she muttered.

Benjamin started up the stairs and winced when he put pressure on his left leg. "One of those guys must've been wearing horseshoes."

There were enough rooms on the second floor to accommodate the entire Maple Leafs team. When Benjamin opened a door to what Alex assumed would be a bedroom, another set of stairs, very narrow, faced them.

"My room's in the attic. Took me three summers to talk them into it. More privacy."

Alex looked around. This was perfect. Who'd want to live anywhere else? They were in a large loft with a dormer window that overlooked the front yard and a half-moon window with a view of the back fields. Shelves crammed with books reached from floor to ceiling next to the bed. Across one wall was a stereo system that looked like it could blast the polish off a gymnasium floor.

Blue-painted walls were covered with posters — mostly of rock groups, but also a full-length one of a discouraged-looking old man with two hands stuffed into his trenchcoat pockets and wisps of gray hair poking out from under his knitted toque. He looked vaguely familiar. Benjamin had rigged that poster himself by cutting a slit on the top of the guy's coat pocket and slipping in a cardboard protest sign with *LOSE THE CRUISE* scribbled on it.

"Who's that?"

"Einstein."

"Oh yeah, Einstein."

"$E = mc^2$. Basic formula for the bomb," said Benjamin.

"Wonder if he was ever in a real protest?"

"Not like that. Paul and Estella said he wrote a kind of warning letter to the President of the United States, though. Didn't do much good."

"Hey, is that a door?" Alex had just noticed that the Einstein poster was mounted on a narrow door that looked like it would open into midair.

"Fire escape. They put it in when I moved up here." Benjamin flopped back on his bed.

Alex leaned against the black cushions heaped on the window seat. From that vantage point he could see all the way down to where the Holbrooks' driveway met the main road, about half a kilometer away.

"What do you think'll happen to those guys," he asked.

"Probation. That won't bother them though."

"My Dad'd kill me if I got put on probation, or even anything near it. If he even finds out about those guys beating us up it'll be a big production and somehow he'll wind up blaming me for the whole thing."

"You get in trouble a lot?"

"Not real trouble."

"So what's your old man so paranoid about?"

"Something to do with my mother. She died

when I was four. Dad figures he owes her a perfect son, or something like that. He grounds me for the least thing."

"If you're good, you can chew gum on Fridays."

"Huh?"

Benjamin pointed to the ceiling.

Alex looked up to see what he was pointing at. Above the bed was a homemade poster with the words *IF YOU'RE GOOD, YOU CAN CHEW GUM ON FRIDAYS* in bright pink, purple and royal blue lettering.

"What's that supposed to mean?"

"My teacher in grade seven said it. We were all acting like goons. Some kids were shooting paper spitballs through the barrels of their pens and making sounds with their sneakers against their seats so it would sound like someone laid a big one."

Alex broke up laughing.

"So Mrs. Corbin gives us the usual lecture. Only this time she ends up with, 'If you're good, you can chew gum on Fridays.' I had a mouthful of strawberry bubblegum while she was saying it! And I wasn't the only one."

"So why did you make the poster?"

"As a kind of reminder. Some rules don't mean anything."

"Hey, is that why you sell grass? Because you think rules are stupid?"

"Never really thought about it. I just started my garden for something to do. This guy at the shopping center offered me a bunch of seeds for five bucks one day and I took them. I didn't expect the stuff to grow."

"But selling's different than growing."

"I don't sell much. I'm not into it seriously. Besides, what else was I supposed to do with the stuff? I couldn't smoke it. My lungs just about burnt out when I tried it and I got real stupid."

"Stupid?" Alex was curious. No one he hung around with ever smoked up.

"Yeah. Like first, I started laughing at anything. I was in my room here by myself, smoking this stuff, and I just started laughing and laughing. I almost threw up I was laughing so hard. So I'm sitting on my bed just about dead from laughing and this stupid grin practically breaking my face and I don't even know why I'm laughing. Then I try to concentrate so maybe I'll get the joke. But I don't. I just feel really stupid. The next thing I know my eyes are like lead and I fall asleep."

"So you never tried it again?"

"What's the use? Once I knew what it was like, why bother?"

"Lots of people do. Till they get used to it."

"Not me.

"Hey!" said Alex glancing out the window. "There's a car coming. Looks like a police cruiser."

Benjamin was on his feet in a second, oblivious of any kinks he had from the beating. "The sergeant! Damn!"

The blue and white car was stopping beside the Mercedes.

"What's wrong?"

72

"Remember that jerk who called me a pusher back at the station?"

"Yeah?"

"Well, he bought some joints from me last week."

"Oh." A picture started to form clearly in Alex's mind. "And the sergeant is beginning to believe his story. Right?"

"Right."

"But he can't prove anything."

"Maybe he's here to look for proof."

"You got any stuff in this room?"

"Not much — and they'd never find it in a million years. But it's not this room I'm worried about. We've gotta go weed the garden, fast."

"Maybe the guy's just here for some details he forgot to ask," offered Alex.

But Benjamin wasn't listening. He already had his jacket on and threw Alex's at him. "Can't take any chances. Come on. Let's get moving."

He opened Einstein's door and headed out onto a wooden fire escape.

"Hold it! Speaking of chances, I can't get mixed up in this grass stuff. Mr. Thomas would send me home for sure. Not that there'd be a home to go to when I got there."

Benjamin paused at the top of the fire escape and turned around. "Right," he said finally. "Put on some tapes so they'll think we're both here. I'll be back soon." And with that, he sneaked down the fire escape.

Alex closed the door. Stacks of tapes were neatly arranged next to the stereo. What a pile of

73

them! He selected one and turned on the machine full blast.

By now the sergeant would probably be sitting in the den across from Mr. Holbrook making small talk. Or maybe he'd get right to the point: "Your grandson is a pusher."

Nervously Alex looked out the half-moon window to check where Benjamin was. He just caught a glimpse of him heading past a clump of trees toward a sort of valley at the end of the field. Absently he walked around the room, looking at the posters. But his mind wasn't registering much. He kept thinking he should be out there helping Benjamin.

Before he knew it, Alex found himself in front of the Einstein poster, opening the door.

As he raced down the outside stairs his heart was pounding like he was running from a fire. But really he was trying to escape from thinking. Thinking of that sergeant sneaking up on him and Benjamin as they stooped like gardeners over the illegal weed. Thinking of Mr. Thomas back again at the police station. Thinking of the phone call home.

As soon as he got to the edge of the woods, he saw Benjamin's garden of tomatoes and Canadian Gold. It didn't look like much — just six short rows with tiny greenish shoots sticking up. Who could tell if it was turnips or catnip or anything else?

Benjamin was busy pulling up every other plant and was startled when he heard the loose stones Alex dislodged as he hurried down the hill. He whirled around, dropped the plants in his hand, and quickly tried to hide them under his sneaker.

"Not such a good cover-up," mocked Alex.

"Phew! It's only you. I gotta get rid of these," he said, picking up the tiny marijuana plants. "I'll dig a hole. Quick. You get the rest of the weed."

Alex stepped across a sparsely planted row, assuming Benjamin had cleaned out everything except the tomatoes. He stooped to begin the job. But which was which?

"Hey. How'm I supposed to know tomatoes from grass?"

Benjamin came out from the cluster of trees, his hands caked with mud. "Right. I'll do this. You get the hole ready. There's a tree trunk back there with a sort of hidden mole hole at the bottom. Stuff the stuff in there."

Benjamin weeded and Alex rushed back and forth from the garden to the hole until all of the marijuana was gone. Then they surveyed the destruction.

"This garden looks like an army of gophers ploughed through. If the sergeant sees this, he'll start looking for what we removed. Better tidy up the rows."

With sticks, they smoothed the mounds and covered up the holes.

"Did you leave a tape on?"

"Yeah, *Greased Dudes*."

"That should keep them away for a while."

"Maybe we can get back before they find out we ever left?"

"Worth a try."

But just as they crested the hill and the house came into sight, they saw trouble. Mrs. Holbrook, with a shawl draped over her shoulders, was walking beside the sergeant, heading directly toward them.

"Oh-oh," moaned Benjamin.

Alex couldn't think.

"There they are! Just as I thought," exclaimed Mrs. Holbrook happily. "You've been showing Alex your garden, have you, Benjamin? You know, sergeant, I never come down here myself, and of course Mr. Holbrook couldn't make his way over this rocky field, but Benjamin toils away on his own and last summer he had a fine harvest. We're so proud of him. Not even the Saturday market had tomatoes like Benjamin's." She placed her hands on his shoulders as if he were about to be awarded the 4-H Club trophy for agricultural excellence.

"I'd like to take a look at this famous tomato garden," said the sergeant. Then he added in a matter-of-fact way that showed how suspicious he was, "Looks like you two've been playing farmer."

Alex looked down at the mud on his hands. "I was helping him weed and straighten up the rows, sir," he said, surprising himself with such a quick cover-up.

"Let's all go see the garden, now that we're this far." Mrs. Holbrook took Benjamin's arm for support.

From the top of the hill it was a peaceful, ordinary farm scene with rows of small tomato plants just starting to grow.

76

"Well, well, isn't this a fine endeavor," cooed Mrs. Holbrook. "Do you have a garden at home, sergeant?"

"Not much time for that," he muttered. From the expression on his face, the boys knew his suspicion was still smoldering. "Looks like something got at your crop."

"Sir?" Benjamin managed to appear puzzled.

"Your tomatoes. Not many of them left."

"That's an experiment, sir," said Alex quickly. "Benjamin planted them far apart like that this year. He wants to see if they'll grow bigger if they get more sun down near the roots."

"If they're planted close together, they shade the lower sections," continued Benjamin, obviously impressed with Alex's lie. "I want to prove that if the stalk gets full sun the tomatoes will grow better."

"How clever!" exclaimed Mrs. Holbrook. "You didn't tell your grandfather and me about that experiment."

The sergeant seemed unimpressed. He began to stroll up and down thoughtfully between the rows. Then he stooped to pick up a limp piece of green. He turned it over in his hand.

Alex heard Benjamin take a deep breath and hold it. There in the sergeant's hand was a sliver of illegal plant. And suddenly it flashed across his mind that lab tests were a lot more exact about distinguishing marijuana plants from tomatoes than he was.

"Is there something wrong, sergeant?" asked Mrs. Holbrook.

He didn't reply. His eyes were fixed on the

trail beaten from the garden to the woods by Alex's many trips back and forth.

Then he did a strange thing. He dropped the sliver of marijuana and dusted the mud from his hands. Benjamin was sure he was going to ask where they had put all the weeds they'd cleared from the garden. He'd been waiting for that question, although he still didn't have an answer ready.

But the sergeant didn't ask anything at all. Instead, he said in a voice that held just the merest hint of a threat, "Well, I guess you won't mind if I check back a couple of times this summer to see how your experiment goes?"

"Of course we wouldn't, would we, Benjamin?" Mrs. Holbrook said. "How nice of you to show interest!"

"I'll save some tomatoes for you, sir," added Benjamin, hardly believing that the police officer could be dropping the whole thing.

Back at the house, the sergeant refused an invitation to stay to dinner. Alex and Benjamin both tried not to look relieved.

During the meal, Mr. Holbrook listened with interest to the story of his grandson's tomato experiment. Alex found himself actually wondering if planting them far apart like that could possibly have an effect on the growth of the tomatoes.

"Why do you think he just dropped the weed and left?" asked Alex when they were back up in Benjamin's room.

"Maybe he figured it was only a weed — the legal kind."

"You really think so?"

"Or maybe he thought there was no sense chasing around just because of one dying marijuana shoot. The rest of the garden was clean."

"Do you think he'll come back this summer?"

"I know he will."

Alex realized that this was the end of Benjamin's Canadian Gold business. "What'll you do? About your business, I mean."

"Nothing. It was starting to be a drag anyway. People were beginning to expect me to have stuff. It gets dangerous carrying it around."

"What'll you do with the stuff you've still got left?"

"I'll just give it away," said Benjamin with a grin, "like some kind of fairy godfather."

Suddenly he decided to make a secret gift to Alex. He hadn't wanted to take grass from some stranger in a washroom, but maybe he'd appreciate finding a couple of free joints tucked away somewhere safe.

"I wouldn't do that if I were you."

"What?" Benjamin was startled. Was Alex a mind reader?

"Something that's against the law."

"Is that what you're afraid of? The law?"

"Yeah. I mean — getting caught. Who wouldn't be afraid?"

"You sure it isn't just your old man you're scared of?"

"What do you mean by that?"

"The way you make it sound, your old man's like Parliament here," said Benjamin. He started to laugh.

Alex barely managed an awkward smirk. Parliament? A crazy thought but true in a way. His dad made the laws and he followed them, no matter if they were stupid or not.

"What you need to do is pitch a tent and stage a protest on your own lawn." Benjamin laughed harder.

Just the thought of protesting gave Alex a weird feeling. That would be the day he could argue against what his father decided.

Benjamin went over to the tapes and rummaged through them. He noticed Alex's jacket on the chair and remembered his gift idea. Without hesitating, he removed two joints from their hiding place behind the tapes and quickly slipped them into the top pocket of the jacket without Alex even noticing.

"I don't know how you do it. All this protest stuff and growing grass and everything. Maybe it's because your parents aren't here to watch every move you make."

"They do watch me. They're pretty good parents. I mean, they know what I'm like and they talk to me about things. What I think about the cruise missile and things like that."

"But how can they watch you when they're on the other side of the world?"

"Well, you know how you always think about what your father would think about things?"

"Yeah."

"Well, I do that too. Only I'm not like you. I don't think they're like Parliament or anything like that."

"Dad's not —"

"I know that. What I'm saying is that I think about them, but I think about me too. That's the difference. What I want counts too."

"So if you want to grow grass when it's against the law your parents would think that's ace?"

"That's not what I meant. My parents know they won't have power over me forever, see. So they tell me to do things on my own."

"Like break the law?"

"Can you drop that for a minute? You got a one-track mind or something? Picture when you're eighteen or nineteen. You'll be so relieved to be out from under the axe you'll probably never even ask your father the time of day."

Benjamin didn't sound like the most rational person Alex had ever met, but all of a sudden, something clicked. The part about the axe. Lots of times Alex had thought to himself that he'd be glad to be on his own in some ways. Not all, but some.

"See what I mean?"

"Yeah. In a way." But selling grass and protesting the cruise still seemed like a weird combination. "Do your parents know about the protest tent?"

"Yeah, they got called when I skipped school."

"Didn't that bug them?"

"Sure, and I laid off for a while."

"But you skipped this week. And not just for the protest."

"I just went over to the festival to see what was up."

"Are you still going back to the protest after the eggs and those guys beating up on us?"

"Sure. Why not? You have to be ready for stuff like that. Tomorrow a defense guy is coming up from the States. Paul and Estella have organized a welcoming party for him he won't forget. Wanna join us?"

"Sorry," said Alex, who figured he'd already been involved enough. "I think we have a rehearsal. Our play's tomorrow night. Hey, wanna go? I think you'd like it. It's about these students who give this teacher a hard time about all the dumb rules she has. They take off out the classroom window at the end."

"Sounds okay. Maybe I will. I never got to see that one in rehearsals."

"Hey, all right," grinned Alex. It'd be fun knowing Benjamin was in the audience watching.

"Guess we'd better head downstairs," said Benjamin as the tape clicked off. "Gran hates driving real late at night."

"Sure."

Benjamin handed Alex his jacket with the two joints tucked away in the pocket. "By the way, thanks," he said.

"For what?"

"Coming out and weeding. That was cool." He smiled.

"Just doing some gardening."

Alex was glad he'd joined the protest and glad he'd weeded too. It was definitely worth it to know Benjamin. Too bad it was so far from Halifax to Ottawa.

*   *   *

As soon as he and his grandmother got back from
dropping Alex off at the dorm, Benjamin went
down to his grandfather's library. "You got any
black paper?"

"What kind of paper, son?"

"Oh, something I can punch holes in. Stiff,
like. It's for a project."

With a stack of black blotting paper and a
three-hole punch, Benjamin headed back up to
his room. He had work to do.

Right now, he knew, Paul and Estella were
preparing the protesters for tomorrow's action on
Parliament Hill. They'd be making new signs.
And Claire, one of the lawyers in the group,
would be telling everyone what they could and
couldn't do.

Finally, with a permanent dent in his hand
from leaning on the three-hole punch, he was
finished. On his desk was a mound of black circles. Confetti. Depressing, funereal, end-of-the-
world confetti. Tomorrow Benjamin would be
ready when the Secretary of Defense emerged
from his sleek, safe limousine.

8
Caught!

Alex was barely back in his room when he was called to the phone. As soon as he picked up the receiver and said hello, Patti started to pump him for information. Mr. Thomas had told the group a little, but Patti and JoAnn wanted to find out the rest.

Alex could hear JoAnn's voice in the background whispering to let her hear too. He had an urge to hang up right then and there. It was bad enough that she was always there. It seemed a bit much that Patti couldn't even talk on the phone without her listening in the whole time.

"Look, couldn't we have a two-way conversation, Patti?" he blurted out.

"What're you so touchy about?" asked Patti defensively. "She's not doing anything."

"I'll talk to you tomorrow. There's nothing else to tell anyway."

"Okay, then. If that's how you feel." Patti's voice showed she was bugged.

He got the message but it didn't seem worth worrying about. "Well, see you tomorrow." He didn't say when, on purpose.

But Patti wasn't satisfied. "When?"

No sense being totally hard to get along with, Alex decided. He wanted to shop for souvenirs on their last free morning. It wouldn't make any difference if he had company. "Want to go souvenir hunting?"

"When?" She was beginning to sound like a broken record.

"How about right after breakfast?"

"Just a minute."

Muffled sounds told Alex that she'd covered the receiver with her hand and was whispering something to JoAnn. He'd been crazy to think she'd actually go with him alone.

After he hung up he went back to his room, exhausted. So much had been packed into the day that it all seemed unreal: the visit to Parliament Hill, the cruise protest, the attack on him and Benjamin, the police station, the Holbrooks' farm, the weed garden. It would take a year to have this much excitement back home.

He stripped for bed, dumping his clothes on the floor. The guy who shared the room with him wasn't in yet. Likely he was in the TV lounge.

Thinking of TV reminded Alex of his father. He hoped all the gory details of the day's activities would never reach his father's ears. It wouldn't matter that he'd been cleared of any guilt. His father wouldn't be convinced. He'd probably say that Alex had somehow started the fight. And never in a million years would Alex want to reveal the fact that he'd met up with a guy who sold dope and had actually helped him to cover up his illegal garden.

"You sure it isn't just your old man you're

scared of?" Benjamin's words went through his mind again. He pulled the covers up and slammed at the pillow a bit to flatten it down just right. But he couldn't get comfortable.

What did Benjamin know? Just because a guy does what his father tells him doesn't mean he's afraid of him. But then again, there were the times he practically tiptoed around the house to avoid one of his father's moods. But most kids did that, Alex figured.

He thought about buying a souvenir for his dad the next day. Maybe he'd get him a beer mug with Ottawa written on it. That'd be a winner for sure. He'd present it when he got back home on Saturday night and his dad would fill it with beer and sit back in front of the hockey game. Maybe they'd have a few laughs together.

Tucking his left arm under the pillow, Alex realized as he drifted off to sleep that in a funny kind of way he actually missed his father.

* * *

The first department store they went into had a whole display of mugs to choose from: coffee mugs, kids' mugs, ceramic mugs with the Parliament buildings painted on them, and finally, the perfect mug for his father. It was a beer mug of thick glass with *Ottawa* scrawled down the side in red. And it didn't cost too much.

While the salesclerk wrapped it in layers of paper and placed it in a box, Alex craned his neck looking for Patti and JoAnn. The store wasn't busy so early on a Friday morning, so it was easy to spot JoAnn and that huge umbrella she always carried with her like some good luck charm. Patti was beside her.

With his souvenir under his arm, he strolled over to see what they were up to.

"Check these out, Alex," grinned Patti, holding up a T-shirt with a whole circle of mounties on horseback painted on the front. "Aren't they too much?"

"Hey, do they come in guys' sizes?" He wanted to buy one for a laugh. That parade of mounties would stop rush hour traffic back home.

"I'm getting this one," said JoAnn, holding up a bright red T-shirt with *Ottawa* written in purple.

"Where are you going?" asked Alex as she headed away from the counter. He already had his money out to pay the clerk.

"To try it on."

Patti watched JoAnn disappear into a dressing room.

"I know I'm a medium," Alex said as he waited for his change. "You getting one?"

"I think I'll look around for something else." Patti headed toward a rack of blouses, trying to be casual. But it was almost impossible to cover up the panicky feeling she had that JoAnn was up to trouble.

Alex joined her and a moment later JoAnn came up behind them.

"Aren't you going to buy the T-shirt?" asked Alex.

"Didn't fit."

Patti couldn't tell if JoAnn had the shirt or not. There were no bulges in her coat. Then it occurred to her — she must have it on. Yes, that was it, because now she had her coat buttoned right to the very top. A small flush stained Patti's cheeks. If Alex found out . . .

"Hey, you guys, look at these!" JoAnn was laughing and holding out a pair of earrings shaped like toilets, white with red seat covers.

"Wouldn't they stretch your ears off?" They looked pretty heavy to Alex.

"Don't be dumb.

"Check these out." He pointed to a pair shaped like telephone receivers, coiled wire and all. "You should get those. One for each of you," he joked. "You're on the phone so much it's practically glued to your ears anyway."

"Maybe we will," said JoAnn. The look on her face clearly meant she didn't think Alex was as smart as he thought.

Patti didn't say anything. She was sure JoAnn was about to try stealing something else, right under Alex's nose! The toilet seats were still in her hand and the carousel holding the earrings separated her from the salesclerk.

"Let's go." JoAnn led the way down the aisle to the front of the store.

Alex stopped to look at some sweaters near the entrance, but Patti and JoAnn kept on walking. When he looked up, they were already out through the heavy glass doors. He started after them.

But someone else cut in front of him. A woman in a maroon all-weather coat appeared to be following JoAnn and Patti. And suddenly a well-dressed man, who seemed to be with her, was hurrying along beside Alex.

The woman reached Patti and JoAnn about a dozen steps outside the store. She put her hand on Patti's arm and said, "Excuse me."

The two girls stopped, and a moment later Alex had caught up with them. He swung around in surprise when the man beside him took hold of his arm.

In a firm voice the woman said, "We have to ask you three to come back into the store with us."

"Huh?" Alex was stunned. He couldn't even imagine a reason for this whole thing. But when he glanced quickly at JoAnn and Patti, he knew something serious must be up. They were both a sick white, and panic showed in their eyes.

Once in the manager's office the woman intoned in a tape-recorder voice, "You have the right to remain silent. Anything you say may be . . ."

The voice droned on. They were being arrested! Alex's head was spinning with questions and the loudest one was Why?

"We are store detectives," said the man. "Do you have anything you wish to return to the store?"

Alex couldn't believe his ears. Shoplifting? They had just bought a couple of souvenirs and — His thoughts were cut short as he glanced up and saw Patti. Tears were already running down her face and she kept staring at the floor.

"Patti?" was all he could say.

JoAnn didn't move a muscle. He could tell she knew something, but she wasn't about to tell.

Suddenly it hit him that he was a suspect too. "All I have is this mug for my father and a T-shirt for myself. I paid for them. The slips are in the bags somewhere, if you just look." His heart was pounding as if he'd already been found guilty.

Still JoAnn sat without moving. "I didn't take anything," she said.

Patti continued to cry silently.

"We'll have to call your parents. You may as well know now, we can get permission to search you."

That's when JoAnn broke. "Patti didn't know about any of this. Neither did Alex. I — I just took a T-shirt." She lifted her sweater and underneath was the red shirt she'd said didn't fit her.

The woman detective took JoAnn to a washroom so she could remove the T-shirt. Alex tried to grasp what was happening. "I don't believe this," he muttered.

"She doesn't really take things," said Patti, "I mean, it wasn't serious. It was just like acting, she said."

The detective had gone through the two parcels Alex had given him and was satisfied that nothing in them had been stolen. "Would you take off your jacket, please."

"What for, sir?" Alex tried to remain cool and polite.

"We have to be sure you have nothing in your pockets."

Alex held open the two side pockets. They were empty.

"Please, do as I say," the man said firmly.

With a sigh Alex removed his denim jacket and passed it to the store detective. "Go ahead, but you won't find anything."

JoAnn came back into the office, the red T-shirt in her hand, as the detective was checking the top lefthand pocket. It was also empty. Then he turned the jacket around to the last pocket and reached inside.

"What's this?" He pulled out two crushed, tightly-rolled marijuana joints.

Alex felt the blood rush from his face. He opened his mouth but could only manage to stammer, "But — I — I — " Instantly he knew that somehow, sometime yesterday, Benjamin had placed those two joints in his pocket. Never in a million years would he have figured a department store detective would find them. But now Alex was framed right up to his eyeballs.

JoAnn's mouth had dropped wide open and Patti was looking at Alex as if he were a ghost.

"We're going to need some phone numbers," was all the man said as he placed the two joints next to the red T-shirt.

* * *

The bells in the Peace Tower had just chimed nine o'clock when a long limousine turned onto Parliament Hill. The protest tent that had been there for months was no longer on the lawn. Its place was marked by a large patch of flattened grass. Benjamin could see Paul and Estella

91

among the other cruise protesters gathered at the side of the drive.

Some cameramen and reporters stood waiting for the Secretary of Defense to emerge from the car. Soon, if Paul and Estella's plan worked, their attention would be focused on the protesters instead. Benjamin wouldn't have missed this for anything.

As the long gray car neared the group, several people threw themselves down flat on their backs right in its path. The driver slammed on his brakes and the car jerked to a sudden stop. Instantly plainclothes men and mounties swarmed onto the scene, lifting the protesters out of the way as if they were sacks of potatoes. Soon the car continued its approach to Centre Block.

Two mounties stood at attention under the sculpted unicorn that guarded the east door. Benjamin smiled at them, while in his pockets he clutched fistfuls of black confetti.

Just as the sleek limo rounded the last corner of the drive the Prime Minister and his aides appeared through the door.

Some of the black confetti stuck to Benjamin's sweaty palms as he got ready. The limo stopped. A mountie moved forward to open the door for the man inside. Standing on the bottom step, the Prime Minister extended his hand in welcome. Cameras flashed.

Benjamin eased down one step. Television cameras were rolling, recording everything. The two politicians were side by side now as they turned to proceed up the steps.

No one was watching Benjamin as the small

crowd of reporters clustered around, poking microphones and shouting questions. He was close enough that he could see the small coin-sized shiny spot showing at the crown of the American's head.

Now!

In a flash his fists were out of his two pockets, flinging black confetti into the air. It scattered, settling on the American's hair, his small bald spot, his shoulders and his hands. A few black circles fell on the Prime Minister and flecked the faces and microphones of the reporters. It had taken only a few suspended seconds.

Then, without hesitation, Benjamin stuffed his hands into his pockets to reload. Another black cloud swirled down.

His shoulders were gripped by two fiercely firm hands and suddenly he became aware of the sounds around him — shouts and exclamations of surprise. The American frantically brushed at the offending black dots, a look of panic on his face.

"It's just paper."

"Where'd that kid come from?"

"Get that camera over here."

The Secretary of Defense and the Prime Minister were hurried into the marble sanctity of the Centre Block hall.

Benjamin watched the dark eyes of the cameras pointed at him. Then, controlled like a puppet by the two firm hands, he found himself in the back seat of a car heading away from the chaotic scene on Parliament Hill. His heart was thudding. Two pieces of black confetti were still stuck to the palms of his hands and he picked them off. He was scared. Yet he felt a feeling of release too. He'd done it!

Something was going to happen to him now, for sure. There would be a phone call and his grandparents would, once again, have to go to the police station. His parents wouldn't like this Sunday night's news.

Soon, television journalists would explain what the cameras had recorded just moments ago.

* * *

When JoAnn heard the store detective describing the situation to Mr. Thomas over the phone, she began to cry. She knew her chances of landing the best-actress award at the National Drama Festival were finished. Her shoplifting meant a ticket home on the next flight.

Alex's thoughts were just as dismal. First Mr. Thomas had to rescue him from the police station when they'd been beat up — and now this. Things couldn't be worse! One thing he knew for sure — when the curtain went up that night he wouldn't be the one with the headphones on, giving all the sound and lighting directions. Lucky they'd trained Carol for the job.

Then a scene flashed through his mind of himself arriving in Nova Scotia and his father at the airport to pick him up. Alex blocked the image. It was too painful!

The look on Mr. Thomas's face when he arrived said it all. He couldn't believe what was happening.

It didn't take long for the whole story to be told. While JoAnn explained about stealing the T-shirt, Alex just sat there. When it was his turn, all he could do was repeat that he didn't know how the two joints got there. It wasn't the kind of line anyone would believe.

The store manager sat back in her chair and thought for a moment. Finally she said, "It's been quite a responsibility bringing these teenagers to Ottawa, Mr. Thomas. It's too bad this had to happen." She glanced briefly at the three sitting awkwardly in front of her.

Leaning forward, she added, "Because of the unusual circumstances, I've decided not to press charges."

Three sets of shoulders slumped in relief! No charges! They couldn't believe their ears.

"I'm sure you have disciplinary measures outlined for such a trip and I hope you will carry them out."

"Yes we do," said Mr. Thomas. "JoAnn and Alex will be excluded from the festival. They'll be sent back home on the next flight, and I'm sure their parents will deal with them as well."

The store manager continued, "I'm sorry to say, however, that as far as the marijuana goes the matter is out of my hands. The police will have to be notified."

Alex thought he'd heard wrong, but everyone was staring at him like he had two heads. He had to go back to the police station — and for something he didn't even do!

"Yes, I see," said Mr. Thomas. "Patti and JoAnn, I want you to take a taxi back to the dorm, then. As soon as I can I'll make arrangements for your return flight, JoAnn."

"Sir," she asked quietly, "who'll do Miss Rule?"

The frown on his face deepened. "Offhand I don't know. We never rehearsed an understudy for that part."

"If I could stay, sir, I — "

"There'll be no staying." He turned to the store manager. "May I use your phone to call a cab?"

"Certainly."

When he put down the receiver, he turned to JoAnn. "Perhaps you'd better go to Beverly Jackson's room while you're waiting for me to get back. Give her some tips about Miss Rule's part in the play. She's the only one I can think of who might do. Of course she'll have to read from a script, but . . . " His voice trailed off in defeat.

Beverly Jackson! thought Alex. As a member of the stage crew she was excellent — fast and quiet. But as Miss Rule? She was just too nice. And holding a script in her hand all the way through the play! It'd be a real wipe-out! Without JoAnn in that leading role, they didn't have a chance of winning the Nationals.

But the Drama Festival was the least of Alex's worries. The two joints still lay on the store manager's desk. When his father got that phone call, he'd hit the roof. There was no way Alex could even begin to explain that he hadn't even known they were in his pocket.

Anger started to set in. If JoAnn hadn't

pulled off that shoplifting stunt! Stupid dumb game!

When the taxi came to pick up the two girls, Alex didn't even say goodbye. Silently he waited with Mr. Thomas, the manager and the two store detectives, for the police to arrive.

*   *   *

Two incidents marked the arrival of the U.S. Secretary of Defense on Parliament Hill in Ottawa today.

Approximately fifty people were involved in a protest against the testing of the cruise missile in Canada. As the Secretary's limousine approached Parliament Hill, some members of the group threw themselves in its path, halting its progress. Quickly and without any show of violence, the protesters were removed from the scene.

A juvenile, whose name is being withheld, staged his own protest, throwing black confetti as the Prime Minister greeted his visitor outside the House. After a few moments of confusion, the two were whisked inside the halls of Centre Block.

Although testing of the cruise is expected to be one of the topics of discussion at today's conference, the cancellation of the program is not likely to be part of the talks.

The small group of protesters later continued its silent parade on Parliament Hill.

9
Police station blues II

Alex sat self-consciously in the back of the police cruiser.

"I want you to phone your father yourself," said Mr. Thomas.

Alex could hardly believe his ears. "But, sir — "

"It's your father, and your responsibility to tell him about what's happened. He'll respect you for it."

"Respect me! Are you kidding? He won't even listen to me, I'll bet."

"You can phone from the police station."

Alex froze. He'd never be able to work out what to say to his dad. He looked out at the people rushing along the street. They probably thought they had worries! Ha!

The police station looked all too familiar. Luckily, the sergeant who'd visited Benjamin's garden yesterday was nowhere in sight. It would be even worse to be questioned by someone wearing an I-thought-so look the whole time.

Justice has a way of working with laser speed. Because his flight back to Nova Scotia was at 7:20 that night, Alex was scheduled to appear before a provincial judge that afternoon. There, the facts would be restated and Alex would likely be released into Mr. Thomas's custody.

He had tried to feel reassured by the words of the officer in charge. Alex was a minor with a clean record. If he'd been trafficking, then things would be worse. He hadn't dared to ask what would happen to someone who gave the stuff away. He didn't want to get Benjamin into trouble.

It was the second time in two days that he had gone to bat for Benjamin and it felt good. Maybe the guy was a bit weird, but there was something about him that Alex had to like — admire even.

"Dial 0 first and tell the operator you want to make a collect call," said Mr. Thomas.

Just the words "collect call" would be enough to set his father off, thought Alex as he pushed the familiar digits of his own phone number.

After five rings, his father answered. He must've been in the middle of something out in the shop. When the operator asked whether he'd accept the charges, Alex could almost hear his father getting uptight.

"Go ahead," said the operator.

"Dad?"

"What's wrong," said his father sternly. "You didn't get hurt or anything, did you?"

"No, Dad, I'm not hurt. There's been a sort of mix-up and — well — JoAnn got caught shoplifting and — "

"Were you stealing?" His dad's voice signaled impatience and a growing anger.

"I didn't steal. I didn't do anything."

"Then what is this? A social call? Get on with it, Alex. This is long distance."

"Well — there was a mix-up and I don't know how they got there, but the store detective found two marijuana joints in my jacket."

There was dead silence on the other end of the line. Then came a snapped order: "Get that teacher on the phone. I got nothing to say to you right now."

"But Dad, I didn't — "

"Do what I said!" he shouted. Alex handed his teacher the receiver.

Mr. Thomas's side of the conversation consisted of nothing more than a few yes's and no's. But when he hung up, he filled Alex in. "Your father's going to wire the money for your ticket and be at the airport to get you. He's doing that because that's what the rules say, but he's pretty upset." He stood up and stuffed his hands in his pants pockets. "I hope JoAnn's parents are easier to talk to than that."

"Anyone's parents would be easier than him."

"You bought the marijuana from Benjamin Holbrook, didn't you?" Mr. Thomas sat down again and faced Alex.

"No, sir, I didn't."

"Why are you covering for him?"

"I'm not, exactly. I really didn't buy it from him."

Mr. Thomas sighed. "Come on, Alex. I wasn't born yesterday."

"I think he gave it to me, sir. Sort of a gift."

His teacher was listening closely now, so Alex continued. "I knew he was selling stuff, that's true. He was in a washroom at the festival. But I wouldn't buy any. Then, when we went to Parliament Hill he was with the cruise protesters and I got curious about him. I mean, there's this guy who sells dope in washrooms and then he's out there protesting against the cruise. You gotta admit that's a weird combination."

"But it still doesn't explain this so-called gift."

Now that he'd begun, it was a relief to fill in the rest of the story. Even the bit about the garden.

"Ah, that explains it. Benjamin started to give away his marijuana supply by slipping you some samples."

"He probably did it when we were in his room after dinner. No way he'd think those joints'd get me in trouble."

"They are illegal," returned Mr. Thomas sarcastically. "Or doesn't he know that?"

"He knows."

"So you're covering for him. Why?"

"He's not a bad guy, sir. And — well, he told me he wasn't going to sell any more. And with that sergeant checking the garden all summer, he won't be growing any either. So I figure he's all through with it. He says the stuff makes him sick so he doesn't smoke it himself."

Mr. Thomas had to laugh out loud at that.

"Glad to know you're feeling so cheerful."

They hadn't noticed the door open. The sergeant who had questioned Alex and Benjamin the day before was already in the room.

Alex's heart started to pound. How much had the guy heard?

"Thought you might be the kid they were talking about. Too much of a coincidence for two kids called Alex to be here from Nova Scotia with a drama club. Getting to be a habit of yours, visiting this police station." His voice wasn't the least bit friendly.

Alex squirmed in his chair.

"Well, I got a bit of news for you." He swirled his coffee in its paper cup. "Your buddy's down the hall."

"Huh?"

"The gardener." He gave Alex a look edged with ice. "The fellow I overheard the two of you chatting about just now."

Mr. Thomas stood up. "Whatever you may have heard is between Alex and myself, sergeant."

The sergeant drank the last of his coffee, then tossed the empty cup into the garbage can near the door. He shifted his gaze from Mr. Thomas to Alex. Then he continued, "Seems he was part of a demonstration on the Hill this morning. With that cruise gang. Made national TV all by himself tossing black confetti at the U.S. Secretary of Defense. He'll be a bit of a hero for that."

Alex wondered what the sergeant was getting at.

"He'll likely just get tapped on the knuckles. Public mischief. Then he'll be back on the street

102

to do whatever it is he usually does." His look got even colder.

"He's not — " But Alex stopped. Better shut up. This man would never believe Benjamin wasn't a dealer anyway.

Then the sergeant said with a smirk on his face, "I hear you're heading back home a bit early. Guess you sort of made a trip all the way up here to Ottawa for nothing. Or maybe it wasn't a waste of time after all. You probably picked up quite a few pointers from that Holbrook kid."

"I'm not sure he has to take all this from you, sergeant," Mr. Thomas interrupted.

"You know, teach, yesterday I maybe would've understood why you'd back this kid. Like I said, I was impressed." He shook his head slowly. "They had me fooled, no doubt about that. Yes sir, I thought I'd met a couple of different kids. Out there protesting the cruise, doing something worthwhile. Too good to be true. I should've known better after all these years in the business."

"Does Benjamin know I'm here?" asked Alex.

"Nope." Then the sergeant stared, as if he'd just had an idea. "Why don't I just go on down there and tell him about your little circumstance? I'm sure he'll want to say goodbye before you head back home on that airplane. He'll be sorry to hear about the possession charge against you."

"I'd rather not see him, sir," Alex said quickly.

"Why not?"

"Well — " He couldn't give the real reason.

103

He knew that if Benjamin heard about the two joints being found he'd tell the whole truth. Being arrested for protesting the cruise was something Benjamin could be proud of, but if he was also charged with trafficking, then the cruise cause would look pretty foolish.

"That's what I thought," said the sergeant. "There's no reason at all why your buddy shouldn't know about your troubles." He left the room.

"Look, Alex, I can see what you're doing and I admire you for it," said Mr. Thomas. "You're taking the rap for Benjamin so his protest won't suffer. But the fact is you didn't do anything wrong. You should be at that performance tonight. And if you're flown home with this possession charge still in place your father will — "

"Kill me," Alex finished. "But you don't understand, sir. Dad'll kill me anyway. You just don't know him."

"But — "

"Nothing'll change what's going to happen between me and my dad, so what's the use of messing things up for Benjamin and what he did on TV? He'll look real stupid if it gets out about the grass."

"What about the performance tonight?"

"We trained Carol. She'll be fine."

Mr. Thomas saw in Alex's eyes that he wasn't about to change his mind.

"Sorry, sir. But it's the least I can do now. It'll make me feel like I did something good on this trip anyway."

The door opened again and the sergeant

returned with Benjamin. "Got a visitor. He already told us about his gift to you, so your game's over."

Alex tried to smile at his friend. "You shouldn't have. We heard about the confetti and you being on TV. This'll ruin it all. Besides, it's no big deal going home."

"Right. And I bet your old man's as happy as Santa Claus that you got caught with two joints," said Benjamin. His smile didn't quite come together either.

"Too late for tears now," sneered the sergeant. "We'll have a signed statement as soon as your grandparents get here."

"You didn't tell about — "

Benjamin cut him off. "I told all there was to tell — that I had some joints and wanted to give my buddy from Nova Scotia a present."

Alex suppressed a smile. The sergeant would have trouble proving anything about the garden.

Mr. Thomas got up from his chair. "As I understand it," he said, "criminal acts committed by minors are not allowed to be publicized. Not in the newspapers or on television or anywhere."

Alex and Benjamin both stared at him. What was he getting at?

The sergeant seemed to know. "That's right, Mr. Thomas. We won't be able to tell the country their peace hero is mixed up with dope, but we can put him on probation long enough to keep him away from more young kids. That'll mean an end to his little business."

"I'd like to use your telephone again, if I

may." Mr. Thomas turned to Alex. "We should let your father know right away. This time I'll call."

"Thanks, sir. But don't be surprised if he isn't too thrilled with the news. Like I said, you don't know Dad."

Even so, Alex began to relax a little. Things weren't exactly roses for Benjamin, but at least he wouldn't make a laughing stock of the cruise cause. And the "little business" the sergeant referred to was already history anyway.

Finally it began to sink in. He was off the hook. How could they charge him with possession when he didn't even know he had the stuff on him?

He'd still have to deal with his father when the Drama Club got back home on Saturday, but he wouldn't have to be on that flight with JoAnn. When the houselights faded to black later that night, it would be Alex's voice whispering, "Cue lights one."

*   *   *

After the woman at the reception desk had paged Patti, Alex sauntered over to the large red leather sofa to wait. She was probably helping JoAnn pack. Maybe JoAnn was a pain, but he still felt sorry that she had to go home. She wasn't a real criminal — just dumb.

Patti got off the elevator alone.

"Hi."

"Hi," said Alex, standing up. "How's JoAnn?"

"Pretty awful." Patti looked down at her sneakers and pushed her fists into the pockets of

106

her baggy sweater. Then she looked up at Alex, almost defiantly. "I'm going to the airport with her."

"Yeah?"

"I know that bugs you."

"Hey, wait a minute. Why should it?"

"You don't like when I do things with JoAnn. And since she almost got you in all that trouble —"

"Look, JoAnn did a stupid thing. And I'm not saying I wasn't miffed for a while, but what's that got to do with it right now? I just came over here to see how things are going and you act like we're having some kind of fight or something."

"You've been bugged about me and JoAnn this whole trip."

"The only thing that gets to me is that you two are always together every single minute of every single day."

"You don't know what it's like," she said with exasperation.

"What what's like?"

"Look, JoAnn's been my friend ever since I can remember. Just because I met you at the Drama Club, am I supposed to drop my very best friend?"

"You don't have to drop her," Alex said. "But does she have to be with you all the time? It gets to be a drag."

"You want to break up with me, don't you?" Patti said.

"How can we break up when we haven't exactly been going together?" He tried to get a small laugh out of that, but she didn't even smile.

107

"I don't want to break up with you," she said. She looked down at her sneakers again.

"Let's start over. Let's give it a try, just you and me."

"But I still have to be JoAnn's friend. I'm not going to just drop her."

"I'm not saying that. I'm just saying that sometimes you'll be with her and sometimes you'll be with me."

"And sometimes with both of you?"

Alex didn't relish the idea of being with JoAnn much, but this wasn't the time to say so. "Sometimes," he agreed.

"Okay," said Patti. Then she added, "Mr. Thomas is taking us to the airport. Guess I better go." She wasn't exactly smiling, but she didn't look as upset as she had a few minutes ago.

Alex leaned over and gave her a small kiss. "See ya later."

This time Patti smiled, though faintly.

"Tell JoAnn I feel bad about her missing tonight. I mean it."

*   *   *

"You two wait here. I'll get the boarding pass," said Mr. Thomas.

JoAnn plunked her backpack on the seat beside Patti. "Look after this."

"Where are you going?"

"Just over there."

When she got to the large garbage can, JoAnn stared at it for a minute. Then, with determination, she stuffed the blue and yellow umbrella in and walked back to sit beside Patti.

108

Neither of them spoke for a while. Then Patti said, "I know you didn't really mean it like stealing."

Mr. Thomas approached. "Your plane doesn't leave for one hour," he said, handing the ticket over to her, "but you'll be boarding at gate 14 soon. It's 6:20 now." Then he seemed lost for words.

"I know you have to leave, sir," said JoAnn. "I'll be all right, really. They need you back at the theater. You too, Patti." She choked back the tears but her eyes glistened wetly.

Patti started to cry.

"It was so stupid," said JoAnn.

"It sure was," replied Mr. Thomas simply. Reaching out, he put his hand on her shoulder and added, "We'll miss your Miss Rule tonight. You would've been tops."

Now JoAnn couldn't keep the tears from slipping down her cheeks. "I'll never get a chance like this again. I wanted to be an actress so much."

"Now, now. This is just one festival. There'll be others. Nothing can take away the fact that you've got talent, JoAnn. And if you've learned from this — "

"I'll never do such a stupid thing again. Ever. I can't believe I was so dense."

"Well, the ordeal is almost over now. When you meet your parents at the airport, you'll have to explain all that to them. Now we'd better go," said Mr. Thomas. "Curtain's up in fifty-five minutes."

JoAnn tried to smile. "Goodbye. Patti, make

sure Beverly knows how Miss Rule's hips hook on the skirt so they don't swivel around to the front in the middle of a scene."

All three of them forced a smile.

"See you back home, Mr. Thomas."

The two girls gave each other one last hug.

10
Curtains

Miss Rule dusted the chalk from her hands. The script she held fluttered awkwardly. She walked down one aisle of the classroom and slowly back up another, then checked her script again. By now she was near the window. She looked out. Glancing back at the classroom, she seemed to study every detail. Then she placed the script on the nearest desk and climbed carefully through the narrow window.

"Cue lights nineteen," whispered Alex into his headset, and the stage lights faded to black. Three seconds later, the curtains came down.

Audience reaction was polite. One enthusiastic person gave a shrill whistle, but overall the play had not inspired cheers. What could anyone expect when they'd had to sit and watch the main character fumble with a script the whole time?

The first members of the cast to take their bows were ready behind the curtain, so Alex gave the signal to bring the stage lights up to bright. The clapping continued, courteous but subdued. And when Beverly Jackson came forward as Miss Rule, the audience showed its sympathy for the ordeal she'd just had to endure.

Backstage, Mr. Thomas smiled broadly and hugged people, telling them they'd done a fine job. But he knew, too, that Nova Scotia didn't have the slightest chance of winning.

"Hey, you guys did okay!" said a familiar voice enthusiastically as Alex was packing props and getting ready to strike the set.

It was Benjamin.

"What're you doing here?"

"My grandparents came with me. They're waiting out in the lobby. Just wanted to say au revoir and tell you the play was great."

Again it flashed through Alex's mind that it would be great to have Benjamin as a friend. "You don't have to say that. It was off tonight. You should've seen it with JoAnn. She acted Miss Rule like you wouldn't believe."

"Too bad about the shoplifting."

"Yeah." Alex pictured JoAnn's red T-shirt. It still didn't make sense that she'd taken such a chance.

"Well, guess I'd better get going. Gran doesn't like to drive when it's late."

"Yeah, I remember."

The two boys felt awkward. Three days ago they hadn't even known each other and now, standing there while the stage crew scrambled around them, it was as if they'd been buddies for years. It was hard to say goodbye.

"Hope your dad is cool about everything," said Benjamin.

Trying to picture his father being cool about him being mixed up in a dope deal made Alex laugh. Then he asked, "And what about your folks? What'll they say about the probation?"

"Not much."

Benjamin shrugged, but Alex knew it wouldn't be easy. For a whole year the guy'd be watched. And not just for what he was doing either. People would think there were things going on even if there weren't.

"My grandfather says he and Gran are getting too old to keep tabs on me and Mom and Dad maybe shouldn't leave me for so long every year. They're flying home this weekend."

Alex looked down at the prop he was still holding in his hands. It was hard to know what to say. Benjamin was looking pretty uptight. "What'll you do?"

"Nothing. I mean, what can I do? None of it's up to me anyway."

"Maybe it'll be good having them around. Maybe you won't mind so much."

A strange look crossed Benjamin's face as he watched the stage crew carrying desks past. "Maybe they'll mind."

"Hey, Alex!" came a voice from behind the flats. "I can't get this wire unhooked!"

"Be right there!"

"Well, like I said, my grandparents are waiting for me, so . . . "

"It's been great knowing you," said Alex. "No kidding. I mean it."

"Same here."

"And I think it'll work out with your parents. Really."

Benjamin smiled. "Well, see you around

sometime." He turned to start down the stage steps.

"Check ya later."

By the time Benjamin got to the back of the theater, Alex was behind the flats trying to untangle the mess of wire.

* * *

The plane's engines were roaring practically underneath their feet. Stewards rolled steel dinner carts down the aisle.

Alex wolfed down everything on his tray. When he noticed that Patti didn't finish her chicken, he ate that too. Mr. Thomas donated his cake.

"Are you nervous?" Mr. Thomas asked him.

"About Dad, you mean?"

"Yes. Some people eat a lot when they're nervous."

"I just eat a lot, period."

"You didn't answer my question, though. Are you nervous?"

"Not much." He took the milk container from Patti's tray and drained it. "Thanks."

"You can have the tomato juice too," she offered.

"Naw. I'm full. Thanks anyway."

"What will you say to him?" asked Mr. Thomas.

Alex leaned back and sighed. "If he gives me a chance to talk, I'll probably start with Benjamin and the cruise protest. That's the good part. Then I'll try to get in a few words about how

114

I didn't really do anything to deserve the treatment I know he'll dish out."

"What do you mean?" asked Mr. Thomas.

"He can't do anything, can he, sir?" asked Patti.

"He won't do anything violent, if that's what you guys are thinking. He'll just cut me off. Period. For good."

"That's dumb, Alex. If my father was like yours, I don't know what I'd do."

"I did try to clarify things on the phone, but he sure doesn't listen," said Mr. Thomas. "Maybe I should help you explain when we get to your house tonight."

"No offense, sir. But Dad won't listen to you either."

Alex looked out the window at the billowy white clouds. Every once in a while he could see the ground far below. By now they must be over New Brunswick. Soon Nova Scotia, with its endless trees and dots of lakes and patches of towns, would appear below the airplane.

"Do you think he'll come to the airport to meet you?" Patti asked.

"No."

"But Mr. Thomas already told him you didn't do anything wrong."

"You don't know Dad. Almost being wrong is just the same as being wrong."

"That's ridiculous," said Mr. Thomas. Frustration showed in the line across his forehead.

"Sir? Can I say something?" Alex passed his tray to the steward and clipped the tray-rest in place.

Mr. Thomas waited. Patti was curious too.

"It's sort of like your play. In a way."

"What's like my play?"

"You thinking Dad might change is like how you made Miss Rule change at the end of the play."

"How so?"

"Don't get me wrong. If JoAnn had been there we would've had a pretty good chance of winning. It's the kind of play judges like. Kids acting real bugged about school rules, but still polite like, and then staging a rebellion which the old hag teacher, if you'll pardon the expression, finally joins in by crawling out the window. That'd never happen in real life."

"Why not?"

"For one thing, the students would do something stupid to protest all the hairbrain rules, like pulling down the soccer nets or something like that. Wouldn't they, Patti? And there's no way Miss Rule would crawl out the window and leave her classroom. I mean, not even a teacher like you would do that, sir."

"So she'd never change, even if she saw the students had a point?"

"Teachers like her never think students have a thought, let alone a point. She'd roar down to the principal's office screaming to get the kids expelled."

Mr. Thomas rested his head against the seat and let the sun wash over him. He had a little smile on his face, but it didn't look to Alex like a happy one.

116

"So you think the idea at the end of my play was false."

"In a way, yes. No offense."

"I guess I would like to think it could be that way. With Miss Rule and with your father too."

"Not in a million years."

The *Fasten your seatbelts* sign lit up. "In preparation for our descent into Halifax, please see that your seats are in the upright position. Extinguish all cigarettes . . . "

Alex clicked on his seatbelt and pressed his thumb against the button that lifted his seat forward. He took a big gulp of air and smiled weakly at Patti. He wasn't quite as cool about getting back home as he had tried to make her and Mr. Thomas believe.

*   *   *

The first person Alex picked out of the crowd as he and Patti walked through the sliding doors into the airport terminal was JoAnn, hugging everyone and having a good cry. Some welcoming committee, he thought.

He didn't even bother looking around to see if his father had, by some miracle, come to meet him.

"Patti!" JoAnn threw her arms around her friend. Their eyes were both wet, and for once Alex felt like he wanted to be nice to both of them.

He stretched his arms out and hugged them both. "Hey, you guys, it's not the end of the world."

"We lost because of me!" wailed JoAnn. "I

117

know Beverly tried, but she had to read from the script and — "

Just then Mr. Thomas emerged from the crowd of disembarking passengers. JoAnn rushed to him and her tears started all over again.

Finally everyone had their luggage, and relatives or friends were leading them away to waiting cars. Alex couldn't ignore any longer the not-so-small problem of how he was going to get from the airport to his home.

"Uh, could I get a lift into town with your folks, do you think, JoAnn?" It felt strange asking JoAnn for a favor.

She got the picture immediately. "They'd love it," she said enthusiastically. "You can tell us about the play and the adjudication and stuff."

But not even a good actress like JoAnn could hide the fact that the ride would be anything but comfortable. JoAnn's parents hadn't yet found a reason to smile. And when Mr. Thomas had approached them, they had apologized like they'd been the ones involved in shoplifting, not their daughter.

"Hey, Alex," said Mr. Thomas now, "why not drive back with me? That is, if no one's lifted my fancy car while I was away."

That got a laugh, even from Patti and JoAnn. Mr. Thomas's Pinto looked like a junkyard reject hidden in among the other cars.

Alex was relieved. "Thanks, sir."

The half-hour drive from the airport was a silent one, except for an unidentifiable knocking sound that originated somewhere below the floorboards in the back seat. When Mr. Thomas

118

pulled up in front of Alex's house, it didn't look like anyone was home. Although it was starting to get dark, no lights showed from inside.

"Thanks for the drive, sir," said Alex, trying to be nonchalant as he reached for his backpack and duffle bag.

"Hey," said Mr. Thomas, "what's that on your veranda?"

It took about three seconds for Alex to figure out the whole scene. What was on the veranda, square in the middle of the top step, were garbage bags, two of them. His hockey stick protruded from one. Instinctively, he knew that all of his belongings were crowded together inside that plastic.

"Uh — tomorrow's garbage day," he said quickly, trying to cover up the situation.

"On Sunday?"

"No, uh — Monday is, but Dad always likes to be early." Before Mr. Thomas had a chance to question him again Alex added, "Well, like I said, thanks for the lift. Things'll be fine. Don't worry, sir."

"Look, Alex, wait a minute." Mr. Thomas got out of his car and came around to stand on the sidewalk. "You can't fool me about those garbage bags. That's his way of saying he's kicked you out, isn't it?"

"Nothing subtle about Dad." Alex couldn't quite get the humor into his voice.

"Of all the . . . I'm going in there with you."

"Listen, sir, I know you're trying to help, like you did when you talked him into letting me go on the trip. But it'd do no good for you to go in there now."

"But what are you going to do? You can't just stand out here all night. This is ridiculous. Garbage bags!"

Alex tried to shake off the heavy feeling that was pushing down on him. He forced his voice to sound confident. "You go home, Mr. Thomas. It's been a hectic few days, I guess you might say." All the details of the police station visits and the rehearsals were scrambled together in Alex's mind.

"But he's saying you're guilty even before you talk to him! That man's the most pig-headed — " He stopped himself in mid-sentence, then took a last look at the garbage bags. "Call me tonight. I want to know what happens. If he gives you a hard time, I'm coming over."

"Sure."

"Okay then." He gave Alex a good luck pat on the shoulder. After a few revs of the motor, the Pinto pulled noisily away from the curb. Alex made a mental note to tell Mr. Thomas to check the bolts holding the exhaust system together.

He turned toward his house, but didn't move. His father was home, for sure, because the van was parked in back by the shop.

Alex walked to the veranda, climbed the three steps to the garbage bags and stared down at them. Through the plastic bulged corners of books, soles of shoes and clumps of clothes. The old stereo his father had helped him assemble in his bedroom obviously wasn't considered part of his possessions, he noticed.

Even though it was nearly the end of May, it felt chilly once the sun went down. It'd be even colder in that house, thought Alex to himself.

For a minute he tried to picture what it would be like to have a father he could actually tell the truth to — about Benjamin's garden, the police station, the egg-throwers and the three guys who'd jumped him and Benjamin. But he knew his father would spend the whole time growling about having a convict kid.

Suddenly Alex realized that he didn't want to bother trying to convince his father he wasn't a criminal. It was too much trouble. He'd never be able to do it anyway.

Without knowing where he'd go, he adjusted the backpack, hung the duffle bag over one shoulder and picked up the two garbage bags. Awkwardly he made his way to the bottom of the steps, stopped to reorganize, and then headed down the street away from the darkened house. The garbage bags knocked against his legs with each step he took.

11
Garbage bags and souvenirs

It was almost twelve-thirty when Mr. Thomas decided that he'd waited long enough for Alex to call.

"Mr. MacInnis, this is Bill Thomas. I — "

From the other end of the line came an abrupt interruption. "If that boy's over there with you, you can forget about asking me to come for him. He's got his things. He can get a taste of what life's like out there. You tell him — "

Now it was Mr. Thomas's turn to interrupt. "Wait a minute. Alex isn't here. What are you talking about?"

"He isn't? But I heard that pile of junk of yours out by the door, and when I went to look, your car was gone and so were the bags. He must be with you."

"But he isn't!"

"But — "

"Now you've really made a mess of things!"

"Just you hold on there. This is between my son and me and there's no — "

"And where is your son right now, exactly?

Or do you even care? Those garbage bags on your front doorstep gave Alex a fairly clear message. Who knows where he's gone. I'm calling the police and then I'm coming right over."

He hung up the phone before Mr. MacInnis had a chance to object.

*   *   *

After dragging the heavy garbage bags for what seemed like hours, Alex needed a rest. He knew he should find a place to sit down until he decided what his next move should be.

Across the street was a small restaurant with a couple of tables in the front window. But first he'd have to ditch the garbage bags. It would look pretty weird to haul them into the place. There was a fire escape in the alley. If he hid the bags under the stairs, they'd be safe.

He ordered a hamburger and a pop and sat down and tried to think. But every thought came to a dead-end. Where was a guy supposed to go? It was already after midnight.

He ate as slowly as he could, but stalling for time didn't solve the problem. The garbage bags were in the alley and sooner or later he'd have to get them again. Then what?

Thinking of his father didn't provide any solutions either. He pictured walking back home and standing there with those two garbage bags. No way he was going to beg his father to take him back.

Some other people came into the restaurant, laughing and taking over the two small tables next to Alex. Time to exit.

He retrieved the garbage bags. Standing there at the end of the alley, he wasn't sure which direction to take. The cool night air made him shiver. Rummaging through his backpack, he dug out his heaviest sweater, just underneath the box with the Ottawa beer mug in it.

* * *

The police had arrived moments before Mr. Thomas's Pinto pulled up in front of Alex's house.

"He was wearing a denim jacket and jeans. He had on red sneakers and a red and blue shirt, I think. But the easiest way to identify him will be the two green garbage bags he has with him." Mr. Thomas gave Alex's father a sideways look with more than a hint of anger in it.

"And do you have any idea why the boy would run away from home?" asked the policewoman, taking notes.

"He's ashamed, that's why," said Mr. MacInnis stubbornly. "Got into trouble on his school trip and he's too ashamed to show his face around here."

"That's a lie and you know it. Look, officer, this may look like it's none of my business, but I'm Alex's teacher and I was with him on that trip. The boy was not in trouble. But this man hasn't got sense enough to believe the truth when it's spelled out right in front of him."

"I don't have to stand here and listen to this. I'm the boy's father."

"Even after you threw all his belongings into garbage bags and dumped them out on the front doorstep as if his life were so much litter in your house? Some father!"

"If I can get a word in here," said the policewoman sternly. "You two can argue all night, but the boy's still out there and we aren't any closer to knowing where he is. Now, does he have any relatives in this city? Or any friends he'd go to?"

"Just his Aunt Beatrice and Uncle Jake, and he wouldn't go there."

"Look, I'll get this description out to the cruisers and they'll start to check bus stations and the train depot. The garbage bags should be a giveaway."

The two men were left alone in the kitchen while the officer organized the search. Neither said anything for a while.

Alex's father started to tap his fingers on the table. Then he rubbed his knuckles along the stubble of beard which darkened his face. "Fool kid. Didn't think he'd take off on his own like that."

"Exactly what did you think?" Mr. Thomas was exasperated.

Mr. MacInnis sat silently and stared across the table at Alex's teacher. Mr. Thomas got up and impatiently paced the kitchen. The fridge hummed.

"That boy of yours is a nice kid," said Mr. Thomas finally. "Not perfect, but for sure not the delinquent you make him out to be."

"You're pretty sure of yourself, aren't you? You see these kids a couple hours a day in school and then take them on a trip and you act like you know them better than their own parents."

"Maybe some parents don't pay enough attention to know their kids."

"Oh, so now I don't pay attention to my own boy."

"Then where is he now?"

Mr. MacInnis puzzled over that question in his mind. Did he even know where Alex would go?

"He ever do this before?"

"What? Run away?"

Then Mr. MacInnis remembered. "Yes."

It was so long ago — Alex had been only four. After they had found him at the playground and it was all over, Beatrice had said it was because the boy was lonely. There hadn't been a lot of time to spend with him during all the confusion of the funeral. In fact, Alex had been gone for at least half an hour before they'd noticed. They had assumed he was in front of the TV while they were poring over insurance papers and hospital bills at the kitchen table.

That had been the only other time Alex had run away.

It was strange, but he couldn't help feeling that his son might be at the playground again. He kept silent about it, however. It was crazy to think Alex would even remember where he'd gone when he was only four years old.

"Well?" asked Mr. Thomas.

"Think I'll go take a drive." Without offering any explanation, he grabbed his jacket from a chair and headed out the back door.

Mr. Thomas was right behind him. "Wait.

126

Where are you going? Do you think you know where he is?"

"It's probably a wild goose chase, but I'm going to check it out."

"I'll come too."

The doors of the van were unlocked, so Mr. Thomas jumped in the front seat beside Alex's father before he could do anything to prevent him.

"Where are we going?"

Still he got no reply.

"Shouldn't we tell the police about your hunch?" he tried again.

It was two blocks and across one main intersection to the playground. As they got close, Mr. MacInnis thought for a moment about forgetting the whole idea. The playgound looked deserted. A streetlight reflected off the swings and the shiny metal of the slides.

Mr. Thomas looked puzzled when he stopped.

Through the wire-mesh fence, all was still. With a sudden sense of total defeat, Mr. MacInnis knew it was deserted. No way Alex would take himself to a playground. He'd just never think of it.

"My God, Thomas, I don't know where my boy is." His voice was choked with emotion. He gripped the top of the steering wheel and lay his head on his knuckles.

Mr. Thomas didn't know what to say. He knew that, for the first time, Mr. MacInnis was truly afraid for his son.

Lifting his head from the steering wheel,

Alex's father wound down the window and stared out into the darkness.

"Why don't we go back to your house?" suggested Mr. Thomas. "Maybe the police have found him."

But when they got back there was still no news.

* * *

Alex carried the two garbage bags only a block after he left the restaurant. Then he stopped. It was late. It was cold. And he was losing all patience with the situation.

In his mind he was having an argument with his father. "What am I supposed to do with all my things in garbage bags?" he was shouting. "You think you know everything, but you don't! You can't kick me out when I'm only fourteen. It's against the law!"

His hands were getting numb and the heavy bags kept slipping from his grip. Whenever cars went by, he felt as if people were gawking at him. So far, fortunately, no one had stopped to ask what he was doing out in the middle of the night looking like some kind of garbage thief.

Stopping under the glare of a streetlight, Alex rubbed his aching palms together to warm them up. He blew vigorously on his fingers.

Then he thought about when Benjamin had come backstage at the drama festival to say goodbye. From the look on his face, it had been pretty obvious that he was depressed. Who wouldn't be? The guy knew he had to face his parents about the cops and the grass. But one thing

128

kept flashing like a neon sign in Alex's head: Benjamin *was* going to face his parents. He wasn't planning to run away. And he wouldn't, even if they stuffed everything he owned into garbage bags.

Wandering around all night wasn't going to get him anywhere, Alex realized. Eventually he'd have to go back home anyway. Even his father must have known that when he dumped the bags on the veranda. And if he was going to yell his head off about how his son was some kind of criminal, then Alex might as well face it now. He picked up the bags and turned in the direction of home.

*   *   *

"Look," said Mr. Thomas to Alex's father, "you stay here in case the police find him and I'll just drive around a bit to see if I have any luck. Maybe he might phone."

Mr. MacInnis sat slumped in his chair at the kitchen table. "Sure," he agreed, though he had little hope that Alex would call.

"I'll just be gone for half an hour."

"Thomas?" said Mr. MacInnis quietly.

"Yes?"

"Thanks. For all of it. Before the trip too, I mean."

Mr. Thomas smiled. "Don't worry, we'll find Alex tonight. I'm sure of it. He's got more sense than to actually run away."

"Guess I managed to teach the boy something then," he said with a weak smile.

*   *   *

When Alex got home, the house looked different than when he'd been there earlier that night. Lights were on all over the place, and the van was parked at the side door instead of back by the shop. Knowing that he'd caused some kind of crisis made Alex have second thoughts. Tomorrow might be a better time to come home.

But it was too late to change his mind. Lifting the garbage bags, he headed for the side entrance. Too bad there wasn't some way to sneak in without all the clatter it took to get the overfilled bags through the narrow door.

As soon as he was in the kitchen he turned to look into the breakfast nook. His father was sitting there alone. Some words of the argument he'd thought about having came to his mind. But he didn't say any of them. The look of relief in his father's eyes told him there wasn't going to be any argument.

"Hey, Dad," said Alex, attempting to smile. His throat felt like it had a golf ball in it, but the words managed to sound fairly normal. "I got you a souvenir. Wanna see it?"